Roy Pedersen was born in Ayrshire and brought up in Aberdeen. After a brief spell in London, where he created the first and best selling Gaelic map of Scotland, he spent most of his working life based in Inverness. There he pursued a successful career in the economic, social and cultural development of the Highlands and Islands and as a Highland councillor. He writes, publishes, speaks and broadcasts in both English and Gaelic on a variety of issues connected with world affairs, and with the history, present and future development of the "New Scotland" and its wider international setting. Sweetheart Murder is his second murder mystery in the Dalmannoch series.

Roy Pedersen

Sweetheart Murder

A Dalmannoch Brother Richard Mystery

Pedersen
Lochlann
8 Drummond Road
Inverness
IV2 4NA

First published in Scotland in 2013
Pedersen
Lochlann
8 Drummond Road
Inverness
IV2 4NA

www.pedersen.org.uk

ISBN: 978-1-905787-93-7

British Library Cataloguing-in-Publication Data
A catalogue record for this book is available from the British Library

Printed, bound and distributed by For the Right Reasons,
38 Grant Street, Inverness, IV3 8BN

For Marie

<u>Sweetheart Murder – A Brother
Richard Dalmannoch Mystery</u>

*The body of Colin McCulloch, a young research fellow is
found stabbed at the altar of Sweetheart Abbey. The police
suggest some form of ritualistic killing may be involved.
Brother Richard Wells and Professor Ruairidh Alasdair
Macdonald are not so sure. Colin had upset many people
while researching medieval paganism and a mysterious
group called the Elven Knights. Among those Colin had
crossed were local neo Pagans, a powerful financier,
landowner and wind farm developer, the husband of a
woman with whom he had had an affair, a group of
Christian zealots and others. Might any of those go to the
extreme of murder? And where did the Elven Knights fit in ?
The Dalmannoch team are determined to find out. When
they do they find themselves in perilous waters.*

CONTENTS

THE DEAD RESEARCHER

NORMALLY, end of term was a time for rejoicing at the MacPhedran Institute of Celtic Studies. This year too, rejoicing would have been in order, had things been normal. In the course of his able leadership, Professor Ruairidh Alasdair Macdonald had seen a steady rise in student numbers and exam results were on the right side of the trend. But this year was not normal. Money was tight. He was in the financial firing line.

"Let there be no mistake; its make or break. Either income from research, or conferences, or other sources will have to rise, or savings will have to be made". Such was the ultimatum of Howard Winkley; the university's bursar. He added: "I have just returned from a seminar on university finance in Glasgow and let me say; if the institute doesn't improve its performance, drastic measures will follow."

Located in a converted rambling terraced house in one of the older parts of the Highland capital of Inverness, the formerly independent and struggling institute was established in 1928 by the late Aeneas MacPhedran, the celebrated Celtic scholar. The establishment was now a partner in a confederation of colleges and research institutions scattered throughout the vast Highlands and Islands of Scotland. If the MacPhedran Institute survived, it was to be re-located on a spanking new campus on the edge of the pleasant, prosperous and burgeoning city.

If not . . .

It was half past three as he saw the bursar out. The dismal Howard was always inclined to lay it on a bit thick. For sure the financial situation was worrying. To be more positive, however, the professor's research work in Galloway, in the far south west of Scotland, looked as though it might be close to bearing fruit with the potential for a series of prestigious and profitable international conferences in the offing.

The professor comforted himself further in that at least it was Friday and for once he had no evening or week-end work commitments. A few routine matters to attend to and he could be off home to his wife and family.

He leaned back in his swivel chair, gazed upwards at the cracked ceiling plaster and grimaced. He lowered his eyes again, sighed deeply to relieve the irritation he always felt after a meeting with 'that obnoxious wee man' who seemed to delight in bearing bad news.

His hand stretched out to pick up a silver framed photograph on his desk. He inspected it fondly. It was of a smiling group, featuring himself and others standing outside of what looked like a Victorian shooting lodge – Dalmannoch – which had become the hub of his southern endeavour. As the tension ebbed away, he, recalled with pleasant amazement how this project had emerged following a chance encounter, a year before, with a young monk called Brother Richard Wells and of the bizarre chain of events that had brought about a network of productive contacts and the creation of this outpost for the institute in that remote and unlikely rural area.

Since then, the Dalmannoch building was increasingly used by local groups and individuals. More importantly, from his professor's perspective; things were now starting to come together on the academic front. Good links were developing with universities, institutions and groups within and outside Scotland.

One of the first practical initiatives to emerge out of the evolving academic effort at Dalmannoch was a post-graduate research proposal by one Colin McCulloch. Admittedly Colin was an odd-ball – a loner, not easy to relate to, but unquestionably very bright intellectually. It was not that his unkempt appearance was a matter for comment; there were many, even within the staff of the college network, whose standard of dress was, to put it mildly, casual. It was an attitude thing. Aloof, sneering, sarcastic, judgemental and yet at times engaging, quick witted, amusing; the problem most people had in dealing with him was his unpredictability – not knowing how next the wind was going to blow.

The important thing about Colin, however, so far as Professor MacDonald was concerned, was an understanding of Galloway's early medieval history and archaeology, equal in depth to many acclaimed scholars twice his age. In particular it was Colin's ground-breaking insights into the relationship between Paganism and Christianity during that distant and ill-recorded Dark Age period which especially excited the professor. This was an area of research that he himself had been pursuing and in which he perceived an increasing international curiosity. And it was out of this international curiosity that Professor MacDonald saw future income generation and the financial saviour of the institute.

Thus, out of a strong mutual professional interest, and almost blind to their differences, an effective and even intense working relationship had been forged between the genial, cultivated professor and the disagreeable, anti-social researcher.

And now Colin was on the verge of something big; something to do with a mysterious group he had called the 'Elven Knights'. All was to be revealed in a pre-arranged phone call at four o'clock.

The phone rang. The professor picked up the receiver.

"Yes Jean? . . The police? . . Yes, of course, send them up to my room".

Half a minute later a police sergeant and a constable presented themselves.

3

"Good afternoon sir. You are Professor Ruairidh MacDonald?"

"Yes, I am"

The sergeant held up a sheet of paper with a scanned copy of a business card that the professor recognised as his own.

"And is this your card?"

"Well yes, it certainly looks like mine."

"Do you know, or know of, a Colin McCulloch ?"

"Yes I do, he's a research fellow with this institute. In fact I'm expecting a phone call from him any minute. Why do you ask ? Is there a problem?

"I'm afraid there is Professor Macdonald. The Dumfries and Galloway police have just informed us that the body of Colin McCulloch has been found in a place near Dumfries called Sweetheart Abbey. He was stabbed to death."

DEVELOPMENTS AT DALMANNOCH

JUST AFTER LUNCH on the same Friday that Professor Ruairidh Macdonald was debating his institute's financial problems with the university's bursar, Brother Richard Wells and Frances McGarrigle stood by the front door of Dalmannoch, two hundred miles to the south, taking in the afternoon sun.

"You know Francie, the longer I'm here at Dalmannoch, the more I love it."

"Me too Richard. We're very lucky, aren't we?"

The ex monk smiled, looked into the ex nurse's eyes and stroked her cheek with the back of his fingers. She returned his smile and put her arms round his neck. He pulled her close towards him with his hands on her buttocks. As they kissed, and felt the warmth of each others body, he was reminded momentarily of that occasion just over a year before, when the grateful Frances had placed that first kiss on his lips, after he had given her former husband a good hiding, thus saving her from violent attack – an action that sparked off a chain of events that had in the end led them by their separate ways to Dalmannoch[1]. They linked hands and strolled across the lawn towards the wood that fringed the property. They walked, they talked and they made love in the wood. The pair had never been happier. They were true soul mates. In confirmation, a cock blackbird sang from the gable of the adjacent chapel.

As they made their way back to the main building they recalled how Richard had given up his vocation as a monk and they had jointly taken over management of Dalmannoch, under the auspices of a new Dalmannoch Foundation, thereby saving the property from an

---

[1] For the full story see "Dalmannoch – The Affair of Brother Richard", ISBN: 978-1-905787-68-5.

unscrupulous developer. They had embraced their new role with enthusiasm; firstly, to complete the renovation and redecoration of what had been a disused, almost derelict, Catholic retreat house, and then, to find ways of generating income. They recognised how fortunate they were to have a band of keen and reliable volunteer supporters, without whom the project could never have got off the ground.

There was the Galloway Gaelic Group led by the group's larger than life teacher, native Gaelic speaker, accomplished piper and Church of Scotland minister, the Reverend Donald Angus MacLeod. Although of differing denominational adherences, Donald and Richard got on very well and the Gaelic Group met at Dalmannoch for their weekly evening class. On occasion, the group took over the building for a weekend, and on one occasion for a whole week, for 'total language immersion' sessions featuring inevitable and hugely enjoyable late night cèilidhs. Richard and Frances themselves had joined the group and while Richard at first struggled with the, for him, outlandish sounds, spelling and grammar of this ancient tongue, Frances stormed ahead; Scots Gaelic being very similar to her own native Donegal Irish.

Douglas Gordon, or Duggie as he was generally known to his friends, the Gaelic Group's secretary and treasurer was around most days as liaison agent for the MacPhedran Institute of Celtic Studies. In this capacity he had already organised a couple of small seminars over the winter and a larger spring conference while building up a data base of international contacts. It had been Duggie too who had made first contact with Colin McCulloch and had suggested that this difficult but intellectually brilliant young man could be useful to the MacPhedran Institute and to Dalmannoch. Duggie had also expanded his own accountancy practice by creating a presence for his firm in Dalmannoch to supplement his main office in Newton

Stewart, almost twenty miles away, where he employed Jessie Dunbar his capable full-time book-keeper.

Two other most useful members of the Gaelic Group were lugubrious but successful plumber Gordon Douglas and his striking and talented blond girl friend Suzie Silver. Besides completely revamping the heating and plumbing system, boosted by roof mounted solar panels and thick loft insulation, Gordon was a valuable source of practical advice and help to Richard as he had systematically tackled the renovation of the building.

Suzie worked part time helping in Gordon's office, but had started up her own interior design business as an adjunct to plumbing enterprise. Suzie and Frances had a special bond. Her initiative, a year earlier, had rescued Frances from the clutches of her violent husband and from the vicious drug trafficking Wilson brothers. In fact Suzie had almost certainly saved Frances' life. For this Frances and Richard were eternally grateful. But it was Suzie's flare for design and colour, when applied to Dalmannoch, which transformed the place from a shabby, if well proportioned structure, into an inviting place of culture and study that was both visually striking and magically calming. Suzie's other significant attribute was that she was an active member of the Wigtown Wicca Coven; followers of a dualistic Pagan religion. On the strength of Suzie's credentials and a measure of broad-mindedness and understanding on both sides, Richard had been persuaded to permit the Pagans to hold their sabbats in Dalmannoch's wondrous and richly decorated chapel. In truth the chapel's architectural curiosities attracted a good deal of interest from a range of individuals and groups.

Three further individuals had important roles in the development of Dalmannoch and its owning foundation. These were Canadian businessman Hector Woodrow-Douglas, Chief of the Green Douglas Clan and main benefactor of the foundation. In recognition of his substantial financial stake in the project he had an apartment for his own exclusive use in the east wing.

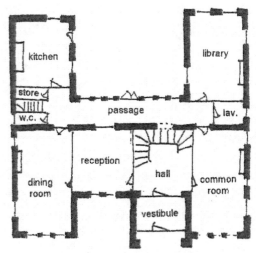

Dalmannoch Ground Floor Plan

Dalmannoch First Floor Plan

Hector was expected to arrive for a visit the following week. Then there was architect Jamie Arbuckle who had latterly overseen the restoration of the building and had ideas for further developments on the site. And finally there was Professor Ruairidh Alasdair Macdonald who in many ways had been catalyst in bringing together several of the key individuals that had enabled the venture to evolve and to progress.

As they considered their good fortune, Frances steered the discourse back to more immediate topics.

"It's lovely to have the place to ourselves today, but I'd better check out Hector's rooms now and make sure they're in a fit state for his arrival. We don't want him to think we're letting the side down."

"You're right, as always – well almost always," conceded Richard with a mischievous twinkle in his eye. "I suppose I should go through today's post. I didn't get a chance this morning."

With that they returned inside to attend to these duties.

As Frances busied herself with making Hector's apartment ready for his forthcoming arrival later the following week, Richard repaired to the reception room, which doubled as Douglas Gordon's office. Duggie had had to spend that Friday in Newton Stewart and as there was no one else around it fell to either Richard or Frances to keep an eye on the communication side of the Dalmannoch enterprise.

Richard recalled his early days at a Dalmannoch lacking both electricity and telephone. Now the standard twenty-first century communication and data processing systems were in place which at times seemed to Richard to create more of a burden on him than when they were absent. He was forced to acknowledge, however, that without such wizardry, the Dalmannoch Foundation could not function viably and develop along the lines that its board of directors had planned.

Having spent a satisfying morning with the, to him, much more amenable task of hoeing and weeding the vegetable patch, now, with somewhat less enthusiasm, he tackled the day's neglected emails – nothing too demanding there. Then there was a smallish pile of post to open – recycling fodder – freebees, offers for cruising holidays, kitchen ware and a chance to win a million pounds (at un-stated odds of several million to one against). The last envelope contained a single sheet of paper. Hand written on it, were the words:

As righteousness tendeth to life:
So he that pursueth evil pursueth it to his own death.

Richard inspected the envelope. It was plain white, bore a first class stamp with a Dumfries postmark and was addressed merely to Dalmannoch, by Wigtown. That was all. How odd – a quote, it seemed, from the King James Bible – the Book of Proverbs perhaps. His administrative chores completed, Richard went upstairs to Hector's apartment to show Frances the message.

"It certainly *is* odd Richard. I don't expect it's anything to worry about. It's just some crank letting off steam." She paused. "We're so fortunate in our friends here, and this is just such an idyllic place, but sometimes I can't help but feel that Dalmannoch is a magnet for odd-balls."

That evening the telephone rang. Frances answered. The caller was their good friend and colleague Professor Ruairidh Alasdair Macdonald.

THE PROFESSOR GOES HOME

AFTER THE POLICE had left his office, Professor Ruairidh Macdonald felt dejected. The looked-forward-to relaxing weekend with his family was on the point of evaporating. He left his office before anything else cropped up to spoil things further.

As he drove homewards in his venerable but beloved green Volvo V70 estate car, he recalled that it had been just a year before that another murder had first brought Brother Richard and him together. Mentally reconstructing the events of that previous summer, Ruairidh MacDonald thought fondly of the remarkable and resourceful monk with whom he had immediately struck up such a firm bond of friendship. It was at Isle of Whithorn, on the southernmost tip of Galloway's Machars peninsula, he had happened upon the distraught Brother Richard. On the previous day the brother had reluctantly headed north, from his monastery in the Cotswolds to Galloway, tasked with renovating the derelict building of Dalmannoch, only to find, on his arrival, the murdered body of Alexander Agnew, the lawyer who was to have advised him.

Despite initial police suspicion about Brother Richard's own possible implication in the crime the redoubtable and personable monk had doggedly set about the renovation project. In so doing he had attracted around him a motley band of helpers and in the process fallen in love with Frances McGarrigle, an alluring dark haired Irish nursing sister, on the run from her violent and cash strapped husband. With the help of Hector Woodrow-Douglas, and after overcoming the brutal attentions of the Wilson brothers, the building was refurbished to become a centre for the study of Galloway's Celtic and spiritual heritage.

What an adventure it had been. Brother Richard had in the end given up his vocation as a monk to settle in with Frances as joint managers of the Dalmannoch Foundation.

To develop a productive focus for these academic links, Professor MacDonald had had to make periodic visits to Dalmannoch, but with the academic and family pressures on him in Inverness, these visits were less frequent than he would have wished for such a new venture. Fortunately, he was able to rely on Duggie Gordon, to liaise and organise things locally on a part-time basis on behalf of the institute.

With these thoughts in his head, the professor arrived at his home with its spectacular views over Loch Ness. He told his wife Fiona about his police visitors and the death – the murder – of Colin McCulloch.

It should be explained that the Macdonald family spoke Gaelic among themselves, but, the discourse that followed may be translated thus:

"Poor boy," Fiona sympathised; "who on earth would do such a thing? He *was* a strange young man, but why this? It's horrible." She gave her husband a hug. "Come on let's sit out in the garden. I'll bring you a dram; then we can have dinner."

They sat together in the garden. The early evening sun still had heat in it. They took in the view over the loch which they both cherished. Their twin daughters Catriona and Eilidh, arrived smiling, enthusiastic and breathless. They had been for an after school riding lesson on the slopes above the loch. Their exploits were listened to with due attention by both parents.

"How was your day Daddy?"

"Good in parts, but all in all, not the best."

"Why?" What happened?"

The good professor didn't have the heart to talk about the financial pressures with which the institute was faced, nor did he wish to mention the "M" word. He simply explained that one of his research fellows had died in Galloway.

The daughters expressed their sadness and asked what had happened. To which the professor was able to state truthfully:

"I'm not quite sure. I'm going to have to go there to see what's what and give my condolences to his next of kin."

"Not tomorrow !" they cried in unison; "you promised to take us sailing. It's our first race."

Fiona and the girls looked at him, as if to defy any backsliding on a promise given. Juggling his responsibilities, on the one hand as husband, father and on the other as troubled professor, he thought fast and confirmed:

"No, no, not tomorrow. Sailing it is."

"Hooray !" was the collective response. Catriona and Eilidh each gave their father a hug and a kiss.

He looked at the pair and at his wife.

"Sometimes I think I'm soft in the head."

"You are", confirmed Fiona, "That's why we love you."

Professor Ruairidh Macdonald, master of all things in the MacPhedran Institute of Celtic Studies, contemplated the immense power of female persuasion and logic and considered himself outnumbered and outclassed.

Over the evening meal Fiona suggested:

"You were going to have to go up (in Gaelic south is 'up') to Dalmannoch later in the week for the board meeting. Why not give Brother Richard a call tonight and go there on Sunday and stay over till the meeting?"

Ruairidh acknowledged that this was a good idea and, once the meal was over, he ascended the stairs to his study.

It was Frances who answered the phone and, after exchanging warm greetings, she called Brother Richard to the phone.

"Richard ? How are things? . . . Oh I'm fine too, just fine – apart from some very disturbing news. It's Colin – Colin McCulloch. The police called this afternoon. They told me – they told me he has been killed. . . . No not an accident. It seems he's been murdered . . . at Sweetheart Abbey. . . I know – dreadful. . . I don't know. They didn't give me any details. Listen – I was thinking on coming up to Dalmannoch the day after tomorrow. Would that be OK with you and Frances? . . . It would? . . . Good. I'll see you on Sunday afternoon then. . . Cheers."

* * *

The weather on Saturday was ideal for sailing with a good, but not too strong, south westerly breeze. Ruairidh and Fiona dropped the twins off at the sailing club for their morning instruction session to be followed in the afternoon by the junior races.

Husband and wife then headed for the weekly shopping expedition to one of the many Tesco supermarkets with which Inverness is endowed. Inevitably Tesco is a meeting place for people from far and wide. They came across a number of friends, acquaintances and others. The professor was well known throughout the Highlands and Islands and he would stop for a chat, whether in English or in Gaelic with anyone who hailed him. In some cases, after a particularly amiable exchange, Fiona would enquire; "Who was that?" The professor would shrug his shoulders and reply: "I've no idea, but I know the face from somewhere."

In these circumstances, Professor Macdonald found the experience of shopping with his wife pleasant enough.

The one fly-in-the-ointment that day was a brief encounter with a sour faced Howard Winkley. The university bursar, pushing a trolley laden with assorted groceries, cleaning fluids, wines and spirits, clearly had no wish to exchange pleasantries, merely grunted at the professor, and pointedly ignored Fiona before scuttling up an opposite isle displaying ladies underwear.

"That", said Ruairidh, "is the university's financial guru. He's got it in for the institute – and, I think, for me in particular."

"What a horrid man," Fiona observed.

In another twenty minutes, they had negotiated the checkout and set off home with the week's supply of groceries, after which they returned to the sailing club to watch their daughters' performance in the afternoon's racing.

The girls were full of it.

"We capsized when we gybed. Eillidh was at the helm."

"It was quite rough, but we managed to right her and get aboard again before the rescue boat reached us. Catriona just pushed down on the centre board, like we were shown, and hauled on the main sheet and up she came."

"We'll have to go now to be ready for the junior race."

With that they scampered off to get their allocated Mirror dingy ready for the impending competition in the waters of the Inner Moray Firth."

The club commodore, Jenny Ross, came over for a word.

"Your girls are coming along fine. They have the potential to make good wee sailors. They'll be at level four in no time. This is their first proper race, isn't it ? The more chance they get to race, the better."

The Macdonalds, feeling justifiable pleasure in their daughters' development, thanked the commodore for her kind attention. Commodore Ross was then hailed by one of the committee members and made her excuses to leave and to attend to her many responsibilities.

Half an hour later the race was under way. The parents followed the progress of the contest. The girls came second, half a length ahead of the third and fourth boats. They glowed with pride at their achievement and on the drive home every detail of the encounter was enthusiastically recalled and evaluated.

* * *

It was early afternoon on the following day by the time Professor Macdonald set off in the Volvo down the A9 for Dalmannoch. He would often vary his route and stop on the way at some interesting location, but on this occasion he pressed on by the most direct road through intermittent showers to arrive at Dalmannoch at about eight o' clock that damp evening.

Richard and Frances' welcome was a warm one, for their shared tribulations and achievements had produced a strong bond of friendship. As there were no other guests that night, a room had been prepared, into which the professor dropped his luggage and returned to the company of his friends. Over supper they caught up on gossip which inevitably majored on Colin McCulloch and his untimely death.

COLIN MCCULLOCH

COLIN McCULLOCH had come out of nowhere. On the wet and windy late autumn day, the previous year, that he had first appeared at Dalmannoch on his small Suzuki 125 motor-bike, it was Duggie Gordon who had answered the door to the drenched figure enveloped, hood up in a soaked kaki parka.

"Come in out of the rain before you're drowned."

The young man entered the vestibule, divested himself of his dripping parka to reveal an unkempt lanky figure, unshaven with tousled mousey hair, clad in battered trainers, beige cords worn at the knees, a grey sweatshirt and a long university scarf.

Duggie ushered the unkempt figure into the reception room, which doubled as his office, and enquired; "Now what can I do for you?"

"I read in the *Galloway Gleaner* that you are going to be running a seminar here in a couple of week's time on Galloway in the Dark Ages."

Duggie confirmed that that was indeed the plan.

In response, the other stated bluntly and without formality, "I have a paper to present".

And that is how first contact was made.

In ascertaining Colin's credentials, it transpired that he was born and raised in Stranraer. He had graduated in history from Edinburgh University specialising in the early medieval period. Since graduating he had been unemployed, apart from casual work in the kitchen of a fast food outlet. Duggie was not quite sure what to make of this somewhat strange individual, but had arranged for Colin to meet Professor Ruairidh Macdonald who was to visit Dalmannoch the following week to finalise the preparations for what was to be the first seminar to be held at the then still only partially refurbished Dalmannoch.

In the course of this meeting the professor quickly realised that Colin McCulloch MA Hons, while displaying an off-putting demeanour, undoubtedly had a well-developed and inquiring intellect. He was especially taken with the young man's focus on the juxtaposition of Pagan and Christian spirituality in Galloway around the end of the first and beginning of the second millennium. This was a topic of mutual interest such that Colin became uncommonly enthused at finding someone with whom he could share his thoughts on what to others was simply an abstruse irrelevance. The upshot of the meeting was that Professor Macdonald agreed to Colin's presenting his paper at the up-coming event.

The seminar itself, held in Dalmannoch's small but exquisite chapel, was a moderate success. It barely covered its costs but it did create the beginnings of a profile for Dalmannoch as a serious place of study. Although the attendance was small, some twenty five people in total, of which about two thirds were members of local groups, historical societies and the like, a number of distinguished academics were also present. This brought a measure of kudos to the occasion.

It was Colin McCulloch's presentation, however, that stole the show. Clear, well argued, he controversially threw a number of new theories into the mix of what little documentary evidence existed to validate his topic: *The Persistence of Paganism in Twelfth Century Galloway*. The academics argued one way and another; they argued about lack of credible evidence, but there was a general acknowledgement that the originality of Colin McCulloch's ideas had opened up scope for new avenues of research. Professor Ruairidh Macdonald was delighted.

On the strength of this, and subject to a vetting process back at the MacPhedran Institute in Inverness, Colin was taken on as a post graduate research fellow. He was based at Dalmannoch but answerable to Professor Macdonald at the Inverness institute, with Douglas Gordon as intermediary. That the professor could offer a number of pointers in taking his studies forward seemed to energise Colin who spent much of his time out and about, no-one really knew quite where.

Colin resented Duggie and tried to undermine his role as the institute's agent in Dalmannoch.

"Why should I report to a clerk who understands nothing of my work?" he sneered, when asked by Duggie for a progress report on his researches.

Duggie did his best to point out the value of team work, which cut little ice with Colin. It required the intervention of Brother Richard, whose authority Colin seemed to respect, to bring about the semblance of a working relationship between the two.

While Colin's academic interest centred on early medieval Paganism, he harboured a special dislike for the Wigtown Wicca Coven, who met intermittently at Dalmannoch. This unusual but likeable group followed a Pagan, or more accurately neo-Pagan, religion based on a reconstruction of ancient traditions, folklore, mythology, songs, and rites from the Celtic lands. Their moral code was governed by the Wiccan Rede: 'If it harm none, do what ye will'. They believed in the Law of the Threefold Return in that a deed done to another person or thing, benevolent or otherwise, returned on the doer with triple force. Their priestess was Holly Garden a tubby, good natured, grey-haired middle-aged woman whom Colin simply disregarded. It was coven member Thomas Nutter against whom Colin vented his spleen whenever they met.

"Nutter by name and nutter by nature," he guffawed. "Call yourselves Pagans? You're just a bunch of hippy pansies, farting about play acting."

An ex-marine; the normally phlegmatic Thomas Nutter, sincere in his admittedly unconventional beliefs, was infuriated at Colin's periodic verbal abuse. He was aware that his surname caused amusement and was inured to that, but such an assault on his creed was not to be tolerated.

Holly Garden, the coven priestess, advocated restraint, but Thomas warned: "That man is anathema to the spiritual craft we revere and, I avow, he will die by his words".

In view of the uncomfortable atmosphere, it was as well for the otherwise harmonious way of life at Dalmannoch that the occasions on which the paths of Colin and Thomas crossed were relatively few and mainly of short duration. It was noticed, however, that in recent weeks the animosity between Colin and Thomas seemed to have died down.

One moderating influence on Colin's derision was his girl-friend Minerva, or Minnie, Skinner. Inevitably, she was known locally, although not to her face, as Skinny Minnie. She had come along to the second Dalmannoch seminar, held in February, at which Colin had not made a presentation but had a support role including leading breakout groups and editing the transactions. For once he behaved in a civil and professional manner; Minnie, Brother Richard and Professor Macdonald saw to that. More academics attended this seminar and the event was considered a success; sufficiently so to risk mounting a larger scale three day spring conference.

This was an altogether more ambitious forum. Besides local attendees, it attracted influential contributors from Canada and the United States, a Norwegian professor and an Italian antiquarian, as well as participants from the various Celtic nations. Among the latter, from Cornwall in fact, was one Angela Trevelyan.

Colin had met Angela a couple of years before at a history summer school in Edinburgh. Then she had paid only passing attention to Colin, but the scholarly, if self-satisfied, erudition of his presentation at the Dalmannoch conference had impressed her. She was smitten. Colin was both flattered by her attention and attracted by her unconcealed sexuality. At the buffet reception at the end of the first day Colin and Angela were observed smooching and giggling together. By the final day of the conference, the pair had embarked on a full blown affair. Had it ended with the dispersal of the delegates, perhaps no great harm would have been done, but that was not the way of it. Angela had a devoted husband and Colin maintained his relationship with Minnie. Apparently, however, the liaison with Angela had continued by email, phone calls and secret assignations at pre-arranged locations. What Angela's husband knew of the affair, no one could say. It did become clear, however, that Minnie had got wind of it and a furious row between the two had been overheard and reported.

*   *   *

On the Sunday night of the professor's arrival at Dalmannoch following Colin's death, Richard, Frances and he reviewed their respective experiences of the unfortunate researcher. They rattled off a list of groups, individuals and causes he had denigrated, either verbally or in letters to the *Galloway Gleaner* – neo-Pagans, Christian fundamentalists, sloppy academics, wind-farm developers, absentee landowners, the London financial sector, banks, shady businessmen, right-wing politicians, left-wing politicians, to name but some.

"Colin was his own worst enemy," declared Brother Richard. "When he behaved himself, he was good company, but too often, he just couldn't resist sticking in the knife."

21

"Unfortunate turn of phrase Richard," suggested the professor, raising his eyebrows. "It seems someone has returned the favour – literally."

"Oh sure he upset a lot of people," Frances butted in, "but who on earth would have been driven to taking Colin's life? It's barely credible."

"Well," said the professor, "maybe tomorrow will shed some light on the matter. I'll have to give my condolences to Colin's mother and make myself known to the police. We'll see what they have to say. As for now, I'm pretty whacked. Bed awaits. Oidhche mhath leibh![1]"

"Oidhche mhath s' cadal math,[2]" replied his hosts and their tired guest climbed the stairs.

---

[1] Gaelic for "good night to you" pronounced Ueech eh vah liv. The "ch" is pronounces as in Scottish Loch

[2] Gaelic for "and sleep well" pronounced ss katal mah.

DUMFRIES

MONDAY MORNING was fresh but dry, the weather front had passed and a high was building from the west. The change in the weather seemed to energise Professor Ruairidh Macdonald for he was up and about by seven o' clock. Over breakfast in Dalmannoch's kitchen he reiterated his intention to contact the Police and Colin's next of kin – his mother.

"I'd better call on the police first to see what they have to say about this sorry business. Inspector Huxtable in the Dumfries Division is the contact the Inverness men gave me. What are your own plans for today?"

"For once we have no plans", Frances admitted. "There's no one staying except you. In fact", she added, "I'd quite fancy a trip to Dumfries myself to check out the shops for summer clothes."

"Well let's all go together", proposed the professor. "And Richard why not come along with me to the police station? You might be able to give them a bit of useful background."

"Sounds good to me", confirmed the ex-monk.

Inspector Huxtable was telephoned and an appointment was agreed."

Twenty minutes later they were on the road in the Volvo bound for the Queen of the South – the historic town of Dumfries.

The car park off Nith Place was the first port of call, achieved after a fruitless circuit of the town due to missing a turning. The car park had an escalator connection to the air conditioned Loreburne Shopping Centre with its twenty one shops inside the centre itself and a further twelve external shops on the nearby High Street.

"This'll do me nicely for a good prowl", Frances announced, and in parody of Macbeth's witches asked; "When and where should we three meet again?"

"Well, let's see," Richard consulted his watch as the trio walked towards the High Street. "Its ten past eleven. Why don't we meet at Kings in Queensberry Street, next to Dorothy Perkins at say half past one?"

Frances and Richard had found this café cum bookshop cum arts and music venue on a previous visit. The rendezvous was agreed and Frances left and went her own way to pursue some serious browsing.

Richard and Ruairidh made their way up Queensberry Street to the Loreburn Street Police Office in time for their eleven thirty appointment with Inspector Huxtable. After five minute's wait, they were ushered by a police woman into an interview room to meet with the inspector and a sergeant.

"Professor Macdonald?" the inspector looked from one to the other of his visitors.

The professor held out his hand. "Yes, good morning. I am Ruairidh Macdonald of the MacPhedran Institute of Celtic Studies in Inverness and this is Richard Wells, manager of the Dalmannoch Foundation in the Machars, which functions in association with our institute. We are both very disturbed to hear of the death of our colleague Colin McCulloch. If we can help in any way – and – em – can we ask as to the circumstances of his death?"

"Please be seated and thank you for coming all the way from Inverness, Professor Macdonald." The inspector's manner was matter-of-fact. He turned to introduce his subordinate: "This is Sergeant John Maxwell. He is assisting me with our enquiries which, are still at an early stage. I *can* tell you that we are treating this as a clear case of murder. As a matter of routine this interview will be recorded."

The inspector paused. Professor and ex monk waited in silence.

"We were telephoned by the caretaker at Sweetheart Abbey on Friday morning. He reported the presence of a body in the presbytery. It had been discovered by a visitor just after the abbey had been opened to the public for the day. As you may know the abbey is a ruin in the care of Historic Scotland and accessible to the public only during opening hours. When we arrived we found a young man's body lying face down across a stone slab where the high altar once stood. When we examined the body, we established that he had been stabbed upwards through the heart. It seems robbery was not a motive. We were able to identify Mr McCulloch from the contents of his wallet and pockets, which held forty five pounds in notes, some small change, credit and debit cards, store cards, memberships, notes, papers, keys and such like – and your business card Professor Macdonald."

The inspector looked coldly at the professor who reciprocated with a correspondingly matter-of-fact: "Yes so I understand."

Inspector Huxtable paused and then continued: "We have not ruled out the possibility of some form of ritualistic killing. I believe your operation at Dalmannoch is a hot-bed of Paganism". He paused again and looked hard at his two visitors.

Brother Richard was the first to speak. "I would by no means use the term 'hot bed'. Dalmannoch caters for a range of spiritual interests. We are not sectarian bigots. But what I don't understand is; who would want to resort to murder – and why? It just seems too far-fetched."

The inspector's eyes narrowed and he snapped back:

"Who indeed? Why indeed? That is what we intend to find out. It would help us a good deal if you could both give me some background about your colleague Colin McCulloch."

The two visitors, who now had a sense that they were regarded as undesirables and somehow implicated, proceeded as best they could between them to summarise how Colin McCulloch had come within their sphere of interest, the nature of his researches and how his personality and human interactions had at times presented difficulties.

When they had finished, Inspector Huxtable expressed a cold and unenthusiastic thanks for their time and information, adding: "If you remember or uncover any further information that would aid our enquiries I'd be grateful if you would contact me. Here is my card."

He passed a business card to each of Ruairidh and Richard. The latter, who had been born and raised in Devon, read it and commented: "Detective Inspector Alexander Huxtable – Huxtable – that's a West Country name isn't it?"

"So I have been informed," admitted the policeman without emotion, "but we Huxtables have been in this area for many generations." And with that he asked the thus far silent Sergeant Maxwell to show the visitors out.

On reaching the entrance lobby, a "Good day to you sirs, I hope you enjoy the rest of your visit to Dumfries," revealed in the sergeant a more gracious side to policing than exhibited by his superior.

"Well," confessed Ruairidh, once out of earshot, "that was more of a trial than I had anticipated. A dry old stick that Inspector Huxtable."

By this time it was quarter to one. "We've three quarters of an hour before we meet up with Frances", noted Brother Richard. "Let's have a look at some of Dumfries's sights." And with that they set off up Loreburn Street and then left to Church Circus and the top of Friars Vennel where Ruairidh pointed to an interpretative panel marking the site of the old Greyfriars Monastery and Kirk.

He explained: "This was where at the high altar Robert the Bruce slew his rival the Red Comyn in 1306. Bruce was excommunicated for his action, but undaunted he began his campaign for Scottish independence. Seven weeks after defeating the English garrison here at Dumfries he was crowned King of Scots, but it took years of guerrilla war to re-secure independence. That was eventually achieved at the Battle of Bannockburn in 1314."

Brother Richard pondered. "Very interesting, but I'm not so sure I want to be reminded of two murders at an altar in the one day."

The pair proceeded down High Street past the three-storey Midsteeple, the fleche topped town house with its carved wall panels, including the Royal arms of Scotland and an external wrought-iron balustraded fore-stair. As they stopped to admire this remarkable edifice placed in the middle of the broad High Street, their attention was drawn to a small crowd harangued by a neatly dressed but highly agitated speaker bearing a placard with the words:

REPENT or face GOD'S WRATH

"Heed my words. The national churches have failed. Their preachers are spineless. We live among the depravity of unbelievers and sinners, but we, the Elect of the Revelation in the name of the risen Christ now commandeth all men to repent and believe. The wicked shall be turned into hell, and all the nations that forget God . . ."

The speaker halted, looked around wildly at individuals in the general vicinity, and then fixed his eye on

Brother Richard. He pointed and exclaimed: "As righteousness tendeth to life: so he that pursueth evil pursueth it to his own death".

The speaker then turned his attention back to the crowd and continued his diatribe and Richard and Ruairidh left the group to make their way towards Kings and their appointment with Frances.

"It's strange," said the ex monk, "but that's the second time recently I have been exposed to that quotation".

SWEETHEART ABBEY

THE LITTLE GROUP at Kings Coffee & Books exchanged the news of the previous couple of hours over a light lunch and good quality fair trade coffee. The men told of the police interview, of Robert the Bruce and of the fanatical street preacher. Frances meanwhile had called at the tourist information office, picked up some brochures about Dumfries and the surrounding area, explored the town centre and riverside and showed off her purchases – a summer dress, sun hat and white sandals.

"Expecting good weather then?" ventured Richard with mock raised eyebrows.

"I live in hope", Frances replied with a playful toss of her head. "And what's more, you could do with something a bit more summery than a boiler suit." She stuck out her tongue at the ex-monk whose work-a-day mode of dress was some way short of the height of fashion.

"While you two discuss your sartorial requirements, and extremely pleasant though it is here, I still have to pay my respects to Mrs McCulloch as Colin's next-of-kin." The professor continued: "I have her address in Stranraer and, as you are aware, that's exactly at the other end of Galloway. It's the best part of an hour and a half away, maybe more if we get stuck behind Irish ferry traffic.

"Sure. You're quite right", agreed Frances. "This is your trip after all. We're just here to brighten your day. Let's press on."

"I was just wondering though", Richard stroked his chin. "I was just wondering if it would be worth going via Sweetheart Abbey – just to have a look at the scene of the crime as it were. . ."

Frances, consulting a leaflet, chipped in: "I picked up a flyer for it at the tourist office and its only seven or eight miles from here".

"Mmm – not a bad idea." Ruairidh mulled it over. "Why not? I don't suppose it would hurt if we called on Mrs McCulloch a bit later."

And so the trio made their way back to the car park; Ruairidh negotiated the payment machine, and the dark green Volvo estate headed south on the A710 to the village of New Abbey in the shadow of the roofless remains of Sweetheart Abbey. They were there in about fifteen minutes and a parking place was found at a hostelry adjacent to the ruined abbey.

"Some place", observed Brother Richard as he viewed the impressive red sandstone building that dominated the village, "and in a better state than I imagined. Let's go and have a closer look."

The three of them entered a gate and made for a kiosk. The professor was a member of Historic Scotland and had free entry, but he purchased entrance tickets and a guide book for Richard and Frances.

Professor Macdonald introduced himself to the caretaker explaining that he was a colleague of the late Colin McCulloch. "Are you the man who reported Colin's death to the police?"

"Aye, that's richt – a terrible shock aathegither. An here's me jiss standin in fur the usual man. He's awa on twa week's holiday. He fair kent when tae absent his-sel'. Mind you a daur say he'll be sorry he missed the excitement. There's nae muckle byordiner happens here fae wan day til the next. I'm Jimmy Grierson by the way."

"Well it's good to meet you Mr Grierson", said the professor. "But tell me when exacly was the body discovered?"

"Nae lang efter hauf past nine when we opened on Friday.
It was oor first veesitor that morning that fun' the corp
lying on the staine that marks Lady Dervorgilla's grave. Of
course I phoned the polis pronto like. They were here
before you could say 'knife' and cordoned the site for the

rest of the day. From what I could mak oot fae the coming and going and me luggin in, I reckon your Mr McCulloch must hae been killt sometime in the nicht."

"Had you seen Colin McCulloch before – I mean when he was alive?"

"Wiel as I say I'm jiss here last week and this, but I believe I saw him here on Tuesday or Wednesday. He wiz a Historic Scotland member like yersel', but I mind he wis kind o' aff-hand wi me, as though he was in a wee world o' his ain. I canna really tell ye muckle mair."

"Well thank you for your information. I have to give my sympathies to his mother later today. It's a help to get some detail of the circumstances of Colin's death."

"Nae a pleasant task richt enyuch", sympathised Jimmy Grierson.

While this exchange was in progress Richard and Frances wandered round the site inspecting what could be discerned of the layout of the buildings round the cloister. As a former monk, Brother Richard was fascinated by this medieval monastery and tried to imagine what the life of the brothers had been like in those far off days. Frances read from the guide book. She noted that the main building, the Cistercian church, dedicated to St Mary the Virgin was founded by Lady Dervorgilla of Galloway in memory of her late husband Lord John Balliol. She was so devoted to his memory that she had his heart embalmed and placed in a silver bound ivory casket. When she herself died in 1289, she and the casket were buried together in the abbey she had founded – hence the name Sweetheart Abbey.

"How romantic Richard – a true love story."

As they moved towards the massive roofless church itself, Ruairidh caught up with them. They entered the presbytery where the high altar had been located. They admired the splendid but glassless traceried windows on the east gable and speculated at the glow of their stained glass when they had been whole. On the ground a recumbent stone had been placed in front of where the high altar had been. On it were inscribed the words:

NEAR THIS SPOT WAS BURIED IN 1289
LADY DERVORGILLA OF GALLOWAY
FOUNDRESS OF THIS ABBEY WHO WITH HER HUSBAND
JOHN OF BALLIOL FOUNDED BALLIOL COLLEGE OXFORD

"Fancy that", said Frances, as she leaned over the inscription, not yet realising the more recent significance of the stone. "They were some couple."

"Yes they were – especially Dervorgilla", confirmed Ruairidh who by this time had joined them. "In fact she founded several other religious houses *and* the first bridge over the River Nith at Dumfries. However, from what I understand of recent events, this is the very spot where Colin's body was found."

Frances recoiled with this realisation which brought them all down to earth with something of a bump. The three of them regarded the site with a greater degree of seriousness. The professor knelt down to inspect the stone more carefully.

"Mmm – there are still traces of blood here – and here."

"How awful for Colin", Frances sighed, herself, as a former nurse, no stranger to the sight of blood. "I just can't imagine who would take Colin's life in this way and what drove them to do it."

The professor pondered for a couple of minutes and then spoke.

"I can't imagine who would have done such a thing either, but we all know Colin upset a lot of people. There may be others we're unaware of. I know he was working on something that he was keeping very close to his chest – something to do with a group called the Elven Knights. He told me it was 'dynamite' and was going to let me in on it on Friday. I need to get hold of his papers and his laptop to see if we can find some clues. I have a sense the police are completely in the dark. With luck maybe we can enlighten them. For Colin's sake I hope so."

After a further silence, it was Richard who spoke. "Right we've seen enough here. Let's head for Stranraer."

MRS MCCULLOCH

MARGIE McCULLOCH lived in a small old terraced house in Seuchan Street in the original Lochside part of the town with a pleasant aspect overlooking Loch Ryan. It was five o' clock by the time Professor McDonald's Volvo came to rest in the street a few doors along form Mrs McCulloch's house.

Not wishing to intrude on his academic friend's duties, Brother Richard tactfully advised that he and Frances would go for a stroll while Ruairidh called on Mrs McCulloch.

The professor admitted: "We don't want to go in mob handed on a sensitive mission like this, but", he pondered; "I wonder Frances, would you like to come with me? Perhaps a woman's touch would make it easier for Mrs McCulloch."

"If you think it would help." Frances looked at Richard.

"That's fine by me love", he shrugged. "On you go. I'll take a ramble round the waterfront."

Ruairidh and Frances walked to Mrs McCulloch's front door. They rang the bell. There was a rustle inside and the door was opened by a woman in her late forties. She had an open face that had not wholly lost the good looks that she would have undoubtedly enjoyed in her youth. Her eyes, however, spoke of her recent tragic loss and perhaps of other past misfortunes.

"Mrs McCulloch?"

"Ye-es."

Mrs McCulloch looked uneasily at the man and woman on her doorstep.

"Sorry to call at this hour but I'm Ruairidh Macdonald – Professor Macdonald – Colin's – er – boss – at the institute in Inverness. I just came to offer my very sincere condolences in this terrible circumstance. This is Frances McGarrigle who manages the Dalmannoch Foundation where Colin was based."

"Hello Mrs McCulloch, if there's anything we can do . . ." Frances was stuck for further words."

"And, Professor, have you come all the way down from Inverness to see me?"

On his answering to the affirmative, Mrs McCulloch insisted: "Here's me keeping you on the doorstep, Come away in. Youse'll be needing a cup of tea, or would it be coffee?"

"Whatever's easiest Mrs McCulloch", at which she disappeared to the kitchenette to the sound of a kettle being boiled and crockery assembled.

The room was plain but neat and clean with three piece suite, television, Formica coffee table and a print of Constable's Hay Wayne above the tiled fireplace. The tea-tray was produced with teapot in a woolly cosy, best flowery china cups, saucers and plates and a cake-stand laden with scones and pancakes.

"I've been doing some baking for the funeral . . ." at which point Mrs McCulloch's eyes filled with tears and she started to sob.

Frances put a comforting arm round the distraught woman. "That's right just you let the hurt out. . . It's all right . . ."

At length the sobbing subsided.

"Who could have done this terrible thing? Colin was a clever boy. He was always good to me and I was that proud when he graduated. Oh why has this happened ? He was all I had left, and now he's gone. Oh dear me; what am I going to do now?"

Frances poured her a cup of tea and Mrs McCulloch rallied. During the subsequent conversation it transpired that Colin was the McCulloch's only child. The father,

Frank McCulloch had gone off with a ferry stewardess when Colin was six and was never seen again. It had not been an easy time but Mrs McCulloch earned enough from a café job and evening cleaning to keep the household together and to ensure that Colin got an education. Colin himself had been bullied at school and had withdrawn into himself. In his second year at Stranraer Academy, however, he came under the wing of the history master, Angus McDougall, or Gus as he was nicknamed among the pupils. History, especially Scottish history, became a passion and, with encouragement from his history master, he started to teach himself Latin to supplement his historical interests. After graduating times were again difficult for Colin with limited income from part-time casual work and no professional opportunities opening up until what seemed like the godsend of the position with the MacPhedran Institute of Celtic Studies.

As the story evolved, Ruairidh and Frances could now understand how a childhood lack of self-confidence, limited finance and a sense of alienation had contributed to Colin's off-putting personality. Yet there was a powerful intellect, tenacity and a sense of mission that seemed to compensate for many of his shortcomings.

By this point the professor sought to change the direction of the conversation.

"You know Mrs McCulloch, I had great faith in Colin. He was developing some very exciting new theories which he was on the point of telling me about before he died. If we can publish this work, it would be a permanent testament to his efforts. Can I ask; would it be possible for me to see his notes and papers and to borrow his laptop – you know, his computer ? It may be too that among this information there could be some clue as to who killed Colin and why."

Mrs McCulloch looked blankly at the professor. "Oh I don't know much about his work. He kept all that kind of thing in his room. The police have already been through his things and I don't think they found much that interested them, but if it would help, you can have another look."

The professor and ex nurse followed the grieving mother upstairs to the back bedroom that had been Colin's domain. Mrs McCulloch had already tidied it up and made the bed. There was a chest of drawers, wardrobe and bookcase, piles of CDs, DVDs and more books, and magazines and a desk with printer – but no computer. On the back of the door was a poster of William Wallace with the caption 'Rebel with a Cause'.

"What a nightmare – where to start?"

There were standard history text books, English, Gaelic, Scots and Latin dictionaries along with a dog-eared copy of Wheelock's Latin, reference works, specialist medievalist monographs and general ephemera. The professor flicked through loose papers, including seminar notes and papers but there was nothing that stood out as being out of the ordinary or useful to the quest. Most of the CDs and DVDs were commercial music offerings or movies but a number were unlabeled.

"Mrs McCulloch, I wonder if I might borrow these. They might tell us something."

"Certainly; if they'll help you." Mrs McCulloch had been rummaging among the pockets of Colin's clothes in the wardrobe and produced a folded piece of paper. She handed it to the professor half apologetically.

He opened the folds and scanned it. It was some kind of list in Latin capital letters.

"Mmm – This could be of interest. I would like to study it in more detail, if I may."

To Mrs McCulloch this was just another of Colin's 'wee puzzles' that he liked to amuse himself with and the professor was welcome to it.

"Well thank you for letting us see this material. I suppose the police took away the laptop."

"Is it not there? Maybe they did, or maybe it's at Minnie's flat. Minerva Skinner – was – his girl friend and he used to stay over there quite a lot. She lives in Dumfries. I like her. She was good for him – took him out of himself, but they seem to have fallen out recently. Colin wouldn't tell me why, but Colin said he was going over there the night he . . ."

"It's all right Mrs McCulloch", Frances intervened putting her arm round the distraught mother; "We won't trouble you any more – if you could just give us Minerva's address. And could you let me know when Colin's funeral will be. I'd like to come along if I can."

With that, the professor left his card. They took a note of Minnie's phone number and address, thanked Mrs McCulloch for her help and made their departure.

Richard was waiting for them by the car.

As they drove back to Dalmannoch from Stranraer, the trio considered the events of the day. It had been Ruairidh who had travelled south for the purpose of making contact with both the police and Colin's mother. It was he, therefore, who first voiced a view as to what had, or had not, been achieved.

"Don't know," he pondered, "but I feel a bit deflated. Duty has been done by Mrs McCulloch although I wish we could do more for her. We have a picture of how Colin died, but not why. And I have a feeling the police weren't willing or able to throw much light on the case either, apart from a theory about some ritualistic motive. So if we don't know why, then we can't know who. Maybe the

CDs or Colin's notes will give us some clues as to his recent movements and contacts.

I think tomorrow, I'd like to pay a visit on Minerva Skinner to see if she has the laptop or any useful information."

MOTIVES, CLUES AND NEWS

B Y THE TIME the trio had returned to Dalmannoch that evening, no one had the inclination to speculate further on the demise of Colin McCulloch, other than a phone call by Professor Macdonald to Minerva Skinner to arrange a meeting the following evening.

After supper, each did their own thing. The professor felt the need to stretch his legs and strode out on a circuit of some of the local country lanes; Richard attended to his vegetable patch and Frances busied herself in the kitchen.

The following morning (Tuesday) breakfast in the kitchen was a leisurely affair, during which Colin again emerged as the main topic of conversation.

In an attempt to bring a degree of balance to the debate, Frances gave voice.

"Sure Colin irritated a lot of people, but, you know, he had his supporters too. He was very much involved with the 'No Wind-farm on Bargieoch' campaign and regarded by them as something of a champion."

"True," agreed Richard, "but I dare say it made him some enemies. Sir Crispin Short is not a man to take opposition lying down. And then there's the Derrydruie development. Colin's spearheading the campaign against that won him friends but has upset the developer and a number of the local councillors."

At this point the professor had to interject.

"I'm afraid you've lost me – wind-farm? Derrydruie? What's that all about?

"Ah yes," admitted Richard, "you won't be aware of these controversial proposals. There has been quite a bit in the *Galloway Gleaner* in the last few weeks. Over the last year, since Frances and I have been here in Galloway, we have explored the area in our free time and kept up with local news. You possibly know that Bargieoch is a moorland ridge in the Glenkens. Well the upper portion of the moor is owned by a man called Sir Crispin Short, who it seems made a lot of money in futures trading in the City of London. He's autocratic and not at all well liked. Anyway he has joined forces with a wind energy company called Beneventus Power that proposes to set up an array of wind turbines on Bargieoch Moor. If the development proceeds, Short stands to earn a handsome rental from the deal, but the turbines will dominate the skyline and will be visible for miles. That's why the 'No Wind-farm on Bargieoch' campaign was established to oppose the development."

"And you say that Colin got himself involved with this campaign?"

"Not just involved Ruairidh; he became one of the campaign's most forthright spokesmen. And I have to admit he put up some telling arguments and statistics about poor efficiency, intermittent operation, high subsidy levels and desecration of prime landscape."

"Mm", the professor pondered, "If I had known he was so involved I would have wanted to know how much this campaign was diverting his attention from his work for the institute. Then you mentioned a place called Derrydruie. What's the story there?"

"Ah well, yes indeed", Richard explained, "Frances and I first heard about Derrydruie three or four weeks ago. There was an article in the *Gleaner* to the effect that an outfit, called Derrydruie Entertainments, planned some kind of theme park on the site. It's fronted by a local businessman called Lang. We went there in the car to have a quick look from the road side. It's what you might describe as a woody glade off a by-road near St John's Town of Dalry. When Colin heard about it, he was incandescent and formed an action group to stop the development and preserve the wood."

Frances had been nodding affirmatively as Richard explained the background to Colin's campaigning activities. She added:

"You will have spotted that Derrydruie is a Gaelic name 'Doire Draoidh' meaning druid's grove and there is a well there, just like our own well here at Dalmannoch, noted, so they say, for its healing properties since pre-Christian times. So you could say that maybe Colin was a bit more 'on message' as regards the work of the institute in this case. Anyway the thing is, that this parcel of land is owned by the same Sir Crispin Short. With Sir Crispin detested by so many in the district, Colin became something of a local hero as a result of his outspoken attacks."

The professor responded

"Well, it's remarkable that Colin has suddenly become a hero rather than an object of vilification, but in so doing, as you say Richard, he must have made an enemy of this Sir Crispin character and his associates. I wouldn't mind a look at Derrydruie myself. How do you fancy a wee jaunt later? We could call on Sir Crispin too if he's around."

Frances announced that she had a lot to do. The following week was going to be busy with the impending board meeting of the Foundation and Hector's visit and other things. She suggested Ruairidh and Richard make the trip later in the afternoon on the way to their early evening meeting with Minerva Skinner – a suggestion that met with approval.

By this point it was mid-morning and each went their separate ways to set about their respective chores. By this time too, Duggie Gordon had arrived. Frances and he repaired to the reception room to puzzle over financial projections for later presentation to the Dalmannoch board in support of future development plans. While Richard busied himself with repair work on one of the outbuildings, Ruairidh read through some notes that Colin had sent him a couple of weeks previously.

Tragic though the circumstance of Colin's death was, this was really a matter for the police to resolve. What was so frustrating from the academic point of view was that the contentious researcher had been on the point of revealing some electrifying new information that may well have made his own name and added to the prestige, and profit, of the MacPhedran Institute. Colin had kept his researches close to his chest, on the legitimate grounds that he wanted to check and double check his facts before revealing them. He had mentioned the mysterious Elven Knights on a couple of occasions, hinting that through them, some fresh light would be thrown on the relationship between Paganism and Christianity in medieval Galloway. But his notes made no mention of this. Who were these knights? Were they simply the subject of some fairy stories that embodied symbolic evidence? Or had they been an actual knightly order, akin perhaps to the Knights Templar; keepers of some secret that Colin had stumbled across? Then again was there a hint in what Colin had said, in his elliptical way, that this group existed currently?

Oh it was so perplexing. Perhaps the CDs might reveal something.

Before examining the CDs, the professor inspected the folded paper that he had retrieved from Mrs McCulloch. He unfolded it. It bore the following hand written lines.

BENEVENTUS VERBEREUS EST
SICUT CHRISTIANI IMPATIENSES
SED MILITES PACIS GALWEDIENSES
CONSERVABUNT SILVAM DRUIDARUM

QUAERITE ARAM BARHOBBLE ET INVENIETIS

The professor scanned what seemed to be four lines of Latin verse and a footnote. Knowing Richard's interest in Latin, Ruairidh made his way to the outbuilding on the roof of which the ex-monk was replacing broken slates.

"Richard, you renegade monk, have a look at this and see what you make of it."

The ex-monk, who was no dunce at Latin, descended his ladder whereupon the professor handed him the paper.

"Mm, let's see." He pondered the list: "It's a kind of rhyme. 'Beneventus verbereus est' – good wind, or fair wind – is – oh let me think – is – is punishable, or deserving punishment, or flogging. What on earth is that supposed to mean? Then, let's see the next line: 'Sicut christiani impatienses' – as impatient – or – intolerant Christians.

Professor Macdonald was impressed.

"Very good Richard. I'm impressed. Can you go on?"

"Well here goes: 'Sed milites pacis galwedia' – but also the peaceful soldiers of Galloway; 'Conservabunt silvam druidarum' – shall help forest of the 'druidarum'? – druids?.

Doesn't make much sense does it?

"What about the last line?

"OK here goes – 'Quaerite aram barhobble et invenietis' – Hm – Seek a refuge, or an altar of – what on earth is a barhobble? – and you shall find it."

It's gobbledegook. Can you make sense of it?"

The professor responded that he had not made any more sense of the rhyme than Richard and that in fact Richard had filled in a couple of blanks in his own vocabulary, but was pleased to be able to elucidate one point.

"Barhobble – that's an ancient ruined chapel in a remote hillside a few miles from Mochram. In fact it's a very interesting place that has Pagan as well as Christian associations.

At this Richard broke in:

"Look its lunch time. Let's have something to eat. Maybe things'll become clearer on a full stomach."

And with that Richard, Ruairidh, Duggie and Frances assembled round the kitchen table for a salad lunch.

"Yes boys. You're all getting fat with too much rich food. I'm going to be strict with you from now on."

Brother Richard couldn't resist a: "Oh Frances, I love it when you're strict."

She flicked him with a well-aimed dish towel.

"Ow! that hurt."

Duggie and Ruairidh said nothing.

Over lunch concerns about Colin McCulloch were set aside. The conversation was focussed mainly on plans for an expansion of both the activities at Dalmannoch and how these activities might be accommodated in new buildings.

As Dalmannoch's most generous benefactor, Hector Woodrow-Douglas, was expected to arrive the following day, the group were keen to have a coherent plan to present to Hector for his consideration and for the forthcoming board meeting to be held on Saturday. After that, all being well, architect, Jamie Arbuckle would be brought into the frame to work up some building concepts for the formal consideration of the Dalmannoch board. In the absence of Hector, however, the discussions were fairly inconclusive.

The participants were starting to think about getting on with other duties when a worried looking Holly Garden, the motherly priestess of the Wigtown Wicca Coven stuck her head round the back door that opened into the kitchen and addressed the assembled group.

"Hi Frances, Richard, Douglas – and oh, you're here too Professor Macdonald; good to see you. Look I'm sorry to butt in on your lunch, but I'm worried about Thomas. He's been missing since last Thursday."

HOLLY TELLS A TALE

EVERYONE AT DALMANNOCH knew that
Thomas Nutter, normally a quiet, composed and
level-headed member of the Wigtown Wicca Coven,
had seriously fallen out with Colin McCulloch, to the
extent that he had foretold Colin's death. Some went so far
as to interpret Thomas' utterances against Colin as a curse
– a spell even.

"What do you mean missing?" Frances enquired of
Holly.

Holly explained:

"What I mean is just that. On Tuesday morning he
said he was going to meet Colin McCulloch and no one has
seen hide nor hair of him since. I have a key to his cottage
and he doesn't seem to have been home. It's so unlike him.
I mean he usually tells me if he's going away for any
length of time so that I can feed his cat."

"Oh my God," exclaimed Frances. "You don't
think . . ?"

"I don't know what to think," Holly declared. "You
know how Thomas and Colin were at daggers drawn – well
I don't mean literally – or – I mean Thomas is normally so
gentle and wouldn't hurt a fly, but Colin really got under
his skin. You know Thomas is an ex-marine and – well –
marines are trained to kill – aren't they?"

Holly was becoming increasingly distressed. She
nervously rubbed, between her thumb and fingers, the
silver circle enclosed seven pointed Elven star pendant she
always wore.

Richard intervened:

"Let's not jump to conclusions. I'll admit it looks
bad but there could be any number of reasons why Thomas
has gone away."

"For instance?" asked Duggie.

"Well – I don't know. Maybe he had some urgent family business to attend to, or perhaps he has had an accident, or . . ."

"You would have thought he would have been in touch with Holly though, wouldn't you," ventured the ever punctilious Duggie. "Shouldn't we inform the police?"

"Hmm – possibly," the professor interposed, "but let's pause and consider for a minute. We have no real evidence that Thomas was in any way responsible for Colin's death – only circumstantial supposition. Do we at this stage really want to trigger off a nationwide manhunt? Richard and I met with Inspector Huxtable yesterday and to be frank, I'd rather put off another confrontation with him until we were surer of our ground. What do you think Richard?

The two exchanged a look that had the hint of a wink on the part of the ex-monk, who, it has to be said, harboured a mischievous streak when it came to dealing with the more officious elements of the constabulary.

"I agree. I remember when I was wrongly suspected of the murder of Alexander Agnew last year. The police were quite heavy handed and unreasonable. I think Huxtable is less than open minded and would be all too ready to pounce on Thomas as an easy target to support his theories of ritual killing. He seemed to have it in for Dalmannoch too. Of course I wouldn't want that to colour my judgement or to inhibit the pursuit of justice, but don't see that leaving it for, say, another twenty four hours would hurt. To cut to the chase, I have got to know Thomas quite well over the last year and I just have a sense that, whatever the cause of Thomas' disappearance, he is not Colin's murderer."

Duggie, still doubtful, listened to this exchange.

"OK twenty four hours it is. Then, if we have no news, I really think we will have to contact the police."

This course of action, or rather inaction, was agreed. Holly was to some extent relieved at having shared her anxiety. After a cup of tea and some reassurance from Frances, she asked:

"Is there anything I can do in the meantime?"

The professor pondered:

"No, I don't think so; not for the present. Let's see what happens between now and this time tomorrow."

Then he had an inspired thought. He was aware that Holly had an encyclopaedic knowledge of local folklore and in the off chance that she might just have some insight not known to the rest of the company, he asked:

"Holly, this is a bit of a long shot, but there is something that may actually have a bearing on Colin. Have you ever heard of the Elven Knights?"

Holly thought for a moment, somewhat taken aback by the strange question.

"Mm, ye-es; I have – if you mean the story of the Elfin Knight?"

Ruairidh sat up straight, surprised at this revelation. He opened his mouth, closed it again, and then, almost stuck for words, gave voice:

"Well – em – I suppose so. Can you tell us about it?"

The assembled company looked at Holly, wondering what was to be revealed. Holly paused, and at length she spoke:

"My grannie told me this story when I was a girl. She told me she heard it from her grannie. It's a fairy story really – very old, I believe. It goes like this:"

"At the back of the Glenkens, there is a lonely moor. Long ago it was haunted by an Elfin Knight. People feared the moor because, now and then, a traveller would set out across it, never to be seen again – another victim of the Elfin Knight.

Well, there were two young nobles, Lord St. Clair and Lord Douglas, who hunted together, and great friends they were too. As the moor was deserted, wild animals abounded there, free from human disturbance, so one day Lord Douglas suggested that the pair of them go to hunt on the haunted moor.

Lord St. Clair, warned his friend of the Elfin Knight and the danger he presented. He added that if they were to venture onto the moor, they would be protected from the Knight's power only if they wore the sign of the Blessed Trinity. Lord Douglas scoffed both of the need for Holy protection, and at the tales of the Elfin Knight, as just a story to frighten bairns.

Heedless of his friend's ridicule, Lord St. Clair plucked a clover leaf from the meadow and bound it to his arm. The pair then rode out onto the lonely moor. There they rode to the hunt, in pursuit of the abundant game. They forgot the Elfin Knight until they stopped in their tracks at the sight of a horseman riding furiously across their track.

Lord Douglas was entranced at the speed with which the beauteous green cloaked horseman rode and was eager to follow and find out who he was and where he was headed. Lord St. Clair warned that the horseman was none other than the Elfin Knight and that to follow would be foolhardy. Again Lord Douglas scoffed at his friend's advice, spurred his steed and galloped off to follow the mysterious horseman, leaving Lord St. Clair behind.

Lord Douglas rode far across the moor in pursuit of the green cloaked knight until he came to a cold and blasted desolate spot. Hoar frost lay on the withered ground. There he stopped, for in front of him a huge ring was marked out on the ground. Within the ring the grass was green and on it danced Elvin figures; their wispy garments curling and twisting like billowing mist. When they spied Lord Douglas astride his horse, just outside the ring, they beckoned him to join them. Frightened as he was, such was the strength of the spell that had been cast over him that he dismounted and prepared to enter the circle.

Before doing so, a wizened goblin approached him from within the circle and whispered a warning to the young noble not to enter or he would be forever undone. The impetuous Lord Douglas laughed aside the goblin's advice and entered the ring to join the dancers. As he approached them their dancing ceased and they parted to form a way through which they beckoned the nobleman to pass. He reached the middle of the circle and there, seated at an altar covered with a richly embroidered red cloth, sat the Elfin Knight himself, handsome and resplendent in his green robes.

When the knight saw Lord Douglas, he bowed and presented him with a goblet. It was filled with heather ale. A great thirst had come over Lord Douglas and he drank deeply of the goblet. As fast as he drank, the goblet refilled itself. At that he realised his folly, but it was too late. His limbs became numb, his face turned white and he dropped the goblet as he fell to the ground, as though dead, before the Elfin Knight.

At that, the Elven host emitted a whoop of triumph, for nothing pleased them more than to entice some unwary mortal into their ring to spend countless years in their company.

Their joy was short-lived. From beyond the ring they heard a sound that they greatly feared. It was the sound of one whose confident footsteps were clearly free of any spell that would normally have been cast on anyone who approached their province so closely. The approaching stranger was none other than Lord St. Clair.

When Lord Douglas had left him in such haste, Lord St. Clair knew that his friend had been bewitched, and touching the clover on his arm, he had set off to try to save him from the spell that had been cast over him. As the brave Lord St. Clair prepared to step inside the ring, the same goblin who had earlier warned Lord Douglas, came forward and whispered also to Lord St. Clair warning him not to enter the ring.

In kindly manner, Lord St. Clair enquired of the goblin from whence he had come. In answer he was informed that he, just like Lord Douglas, had come from the world of mortals. He had likewise followed the green knight to the enchanted ring and drank of the heather ale, as a result of which he was doomed to spend seven years in the company of the Elven host. The anxious young lord, immune to the spell by virtue of the clover leaf he bore, queried if there was nothing that could be done to save Lord Douglas. To this the goblin replied that there was something, dangerous though it be.

The goblin instructed the valiant noble to remain still in the frost where he was, until the break of dawn, then to walk with measured pace seven times round the edge of the enchanted circle. When he had completed the seven circuits, he was to enter the ring and stride boldly to the red draped altar, where sat the Elven Knight. He was then to carry away the goblet of heather ale without spilling a drop and without uttering a word. On concluding this council, the goblin returned to join the Elven host within the ring.

Lord St. Clair waited the long hours until the break of dawn, whereupon he did exactly as the goblin had instructed. As he circled the ring angry murmurs emanated from within the ring and the ground shook, but the Sign of the Holy Trinity kept him safe from harm. As he entered the ring, he saw that the Elves were as icy forms. By the altar the Elfin Knight was likewise an icy figure while the stiff body of Lord Douglas lay prone before him. As Lord St. Clair seized the goblet two ravens swooped and shrieked furiously, as if to retrieve the cup, and loud and terrible were the screams from the frozen Elves. With the Holy talisman as protection the young lord heeded them not and when he passed outside the ring, he flung the goblet from him.

With that, the frozen Elves and the Elfin Knight vanished and silence reigned. All that remained within the grassy ring was Lord Douglas in his repose and a flat grey slab of whinstone where the red draped altar had been.

Great was the joy of Lord St. Clair as he saw his friend stir, open his eyes, stretch his limbs and then stand up to look around unsure of where he was. Lord St. Clair embraced his friend until his wits returned.

At the spot where the goblet had been cast, there was nothing to be seen but a lump of curiously shaped grey stone.

For the rest of their long lives, Lord St. Clair and Lord Douglas were assiduous in their attendance at church and were good to the poor."

The little group in the kitchen of Dalmannoch had listened in silence, entranced almost, as Holly's tale unfolded.

"That is the tale of the Elfin Knight as I remember it."

The professor was the first to speak:

"Well Holly; that was some tale. Whether or not it brings us any closer to Colin's researches or to his murderer, I don't know, but thank you for giving us a fascinating piece of folklore".

DERRYDRUIE

AT AROUND THREE O'CLOCK that afternoon Professor Ruairidh Macdonald and Richard set out in the Volvo to have a look at Derrydruie prior to meeting with Minerva Skinner. On the way, they turned over the events of the previous couple of days. The professor summed up the situation:

"I suppose by rights, finding Colin's killer should be entirely a matter for the police, yet you seem to share the same discomfort as me with Huxtable's approach. Thomas' disappearance does seem incriminating, and yet . . ."

"I just wonder," Richard ventured, "With a bit of detective work at our own hand, knowing Colin as we do, we may be able to point the police in the right direction, minimise hurting too many people and hopefully retrieve some of Colin's research work into the bargain."

The professor was particularly keen on the last named thought, admitting:

"Despite Colin's character flaws, he showed such promise as an academic. If we can rescue his research findings, they could be published as an important and lasting memorial to his short life. Having said that, however, I have my doubts if Holly's tale of the Elfin Knight takes us any further down that road. And yet . . . sometimes these old folk tales have a grain of truth in them."

Past the Newton Stewart junction, the green Volvo turned left on to the A 712 for the Glenkens. In less than half an hour they stopped the car on a by-road beside an area of natural woodland.

Richard announced, "This is Derrydruie".

The two men climbed over a padlocked gate and followed a grassy path into the wood which abounded in native Scottish species – oak, birch, hazel, alder and others

As they progressed, the secluded leafy grove, interspersed with sun dappled clearings resonant with sweet bird-song, seemed to have a calming and bewitching effect. Neither man spoke until after a few minutes they reached a larger and slightly elevated grassy clearing within which was a low circle of stones. Just beyond the stone circle in a hollow a spring issued into a small pool.

The professor was the first to speak.

"Some place! It's almost like Holly's fairy ring, but a more welcoming version. I can see now why it's called Derrydruie – druid's grove. The juxtaposition of mound, circle and spring certainly suggests an ancient Pagan site – I'm not surprised Colin was interested in it. And I was completely unaware of its existence until now."

The pair poked around the site. A large flat stone lay at the centre of the stone circle.

Richard was the next to give voice

"That's strange. There's a white pebble on this flat stone. I wonder who put that there?"

Ruairidh came over to have a look.

"Ah ha, a quartz pebble. Traditionally these round white stones were believed to have healing and protective properties. Our Wiccan friends would use quartz in full moon rituals because it is clearly visible in moonlight and is associated with the goddess. It seems that ancient as this site is, it's still in use for some ritual purpose."

A further exploration brought them to the spring and pool. A few more randomly placed white quartz pebbles could be seen through the clear water outlined against the dark bottom. Hanging from a low bough above the pool had been tied a small piece of emerald green cloth.

Fingering the material, Ruairidh spoke again:

"Mm, that's interesting – silk – and look – it's embroidered with a white seven pointed star. There's one just like it on the wall of the chapel at Dalmannoch."

Richard examined the item and added:

"Yes, an Elven star as used by the Wigtown Wicca Coven. Perhaps one of them put it here. I think we should ask Holly or Suzie if they have been here or if they know anything about the place. You never know, it may even have some bearing on Colin's recent activities or even Thomas' disappearance. But time's wearing on. Let's head back to the car."

THE WARDEN OF THE WOOD

RICHARD AND RUAIRIDH had just climbed back over the gate between wood and road with the intention of making their way back to the car, when they observed an irate figure, hastening towards them with a mincing gait and clearly wishing to have words. He was of middle age, dressed in neat checked shirt with plain tie, fine tweed jacket, immaculately pressed beige twill trousers and tan brogues – county attire, but just a little too perfect to be convincing as belonging to a true countryman.

"This wood is private property. You must keep off. I can't have any Tom, Dick or Harry trespassing on Sir Crispin Short's land. Now clear off and don't come back!"

This admonition was delivered in the accent of the Home Counties, with perhaps a hint of suppressed Cockney.

The professor paused, eyed this individual with a steady gaze and took up the challenge

"And you are?"

The complainant blustered, "I, I, I – I keep an eye on the Derrydruie wood for Sir Crispin – I . . ."

In a gesture of warmth and friendship he did not feel, the smiling academic held out his hand.

"I'm pleased to meet you, Mr . . ?"

"Boosie – Albert Boosie."

Richard did his best to hide a smirk at the mention of the surname of this singularly sober looking individual.

"Mr Boosie. We mean no harm. As you will be aware" (Albert Boosie was not) "there is no law of trespass in Scotland. So long as no damage is done or intended, we are free to walk where we will. However, perhaps I should explain; I am Ruairidh Alasdair Macdonald, Professor at the MacPhedran Institute in Inverness and this is my associate Richard Wells. We are undertaking some research into – how shall I put it – a number of ancient sites in the area, among which some of the features of Derrydruie are of interest. I'm sure Sir Crispin would not wish to stand in the way of academic endeavour."

Albert Boosie had no idea as to what kind of activity the MacPhedran Institute undertook, be it nuclear physics or Chinese poetry, nor did he really care. But, snob that he was, he was sufficiently impressed with the professor's credentials to adjust his manner. Turning his back on Richard, assuming him to be some sort of underling, the said Albert Boosie simpered.

"Ah yes, Mr – er – Professor, I'm sure Sir Crispin would appreciate the needs of academia. You will understand I have to keep an eye open for undesirables. We have had a few incidents here at Derrydruie. In fact the police had to be called quite recently to move some very unpleasant people – hippies, gypsies and such like. We moved to Scotland to get away from such riff-raff and then we find them on our doorstep. It was quite intolerable. Landed proprietors have to be so careful, don't you know."

As Ruairidh listened to this tirade, he was aware that Richard had been blanked by Sir Crispin's champion. In a slightly mischievous and inventive ploy he sought to level the ranking.

"My friend Richard Wells here is proprietor of the Dalmannoch Estate. I dare say Richard you will have views about visitors to your neck of the woods."

"Yes I do. One does have to be careful of course, but one has also to be open minded. We have certainly entertained a most varied and interesting range of visitors at Dalmannoch: people from many countries and all walks of life, who greatly enrich our experience."

This intervention caused a further and disorienting adjustment to Albert Boosie's preconceptions as to the gradations of social position upon which he placed such importance in dealing with his fellow man. It went without saying that superiors, like Sir Crispin were to be looked up to, indeed deferred to. Inferiors were to be looked down on and despised. In this case appearances certainly seemed to be deceptive. The car of these two men was very old, although admittedly of good make, they were by no means smartly dressed, and their strong accents – Highland Scots and West Country. How was he to know that one was a professor and the other some kind of laird? He sought to make amends for his misjudgement.

"Our cottage 'Dingley Dell' is just along the road. May I offer you both a cup of tea?"

To assuage their curiosity, the invitation was accepted. As a consequence the group approached a substantial white ranch style bungalow of nineteen sixties vintage that lay a couple of hundred yards along the road.

"Gertrude ! We have visitors."

At this signal, a serious looking woman with short grey hair and wearing a powder blue twin-set appeared at the front door as the three men approached. She was escorted by a pair of yapping short haired dachshunds. The dogs, Bill and Ben, were ushered into the kitchen. Introductions were effected and professor and ex-monk found themselves seated in the lounge to await the promised beverage. The room was carefully decorated in pastel shades with matching curtains and three piece suite accompanied by teak G Plan coffee table, nest of tables, bureau and, above the tiled fireplace, a framed oil painting of geese in a wetland landscape.

When tea and cakes arrived, the Boosies described how they had moved from the London suburb of Enfield to Scotland in pursuit of their interest in ornithology. Albert had been an actuary with the Vigilant and Secure Life Assurance Company based in Liverpool Street. His wife Gertrude had risen to office manager with the same firm. They had originally intended to move to the Lake District.

On crossing the border, however, they had chanced upon the sale, for a very reasonable price, by The Huddersfield and Whitby Building Society, of the property they now occupied. It had been repossessed from a mortgage defaulter who had lost his job.

The Boosies hadn't made many friends in the area other than acquaintances among the local bird watching fraternity. They had, however, managed to ingratiate themselves into some kind of social contact with Sir Crispin Short by virtue of Albert's undertaking some accounting work for the landowner.

The mention of Sir Crispin prompted Richard to enquire:

"I was reading in the press that Sir Crispin and his associates have plans for Derrydruie. What are your thoughts on that?"

"Our thoughts? Well we're not very happy – not very happy at all. We bought this place to get away from the hustle and bustle of London and now this man George Lang proposes to build a fun fair in the wood almost opposite our cottage."

"And it is being backed by that disagreeable Councillor Norrie Armstrong", chipped in Mrs Boosie. "He's Labour you know", she added meaningfully with a nod.

Brother Richard sympathised, not one way or the other regarding the political affiliation of the councillor, but with the Boosie's concern over the nature of the proposed development:

"Must have been irritating for you. I heard some sort of group was set up to oppose the development. Did you participate?"

"Oh no; we wouldn't want to upset Sir Crispin, would we dear?"

Mrs Boosie nodded in affirmation.

"Oh no dear, we wouldn't want to upset Sir Crispin."

Then Ruairidh had a brain wave.

"I think, as we have invaded his land, it would be a courtesy to call on Sir Crispin if he's about. Is he at home just now do you know?"

On confirmation that the landowner was in all likelihood at home, the professor looked at his watch, rose, thanked the Boosies for their hospitality and the two friends made to take their leave of the ex-actuary and his wife.

They were escorted through the carefully tended front garden, which featured a display of ceramic gnomes, one of which was dangling a fishing line in a tiny pond. A wood-pigeon had perched on the roof of an adjacent wishing well canopy. Startled by the sudden appearance of four humans, it took off, simultaneously evacuating its bowels. The content of this organ spattered on the shoulder and lapel of Albert Boosie's good tweed jacket. It is speculated that wood-pigeons are no longer high on the Boosies list of ornithological favourites.

"Do you know," confessed Richard once out of earshot, "despite their pretensions, that pair are like fish out of water. I feel rather sorry for them."

* * *

The green Volvo V70 Estate swung between a pair of stout entrance pillars and rumbled along a curving gravel drive to draw up beside a silver grey Bentley Continental GT at the front door of Bargieoch House. It was an Edwardian pile of little architectural merit; the country seat of Sir Crispin Short. The ex-monk and professor alighted and approached the front threshold. Ruairidh tugged the brass bell pull. A tinkling was heard from within and in due course a middle aged woman opened the door.

"Good afternoon, I'm Professor Ruairidh Macdonald. I wonder if we could have a few words with Sir Crispin?"

He handed the woman his card.

She, on examining the card, bid the two men enter, urged them through a voluminous panelled hall to an anti-room where they were asked to wait. After a few minutes a tall man with longish wavy fair hair, dressed in faded jeans, crumpled yellow polo shirt and white loafers entered the room. His voice boomed:

"Hellew. You wished to see me?"

"Sir Crispin? – Yes indeed, I'm afraid we unintentionally intruded onto your land at Derrydruie until Mr and Mrs Boosie informed us of the error of our ways."

"Iew, Bertie and Gertie – hwa, hwa – my faithful gahd dogs – hwa, hwa."

"That's not the main reason for our call, however, and we won't take up your time but, this is Brother Richard Wells of Dalmannoch and I'm professor at the MacPhedran Institute in Inverness. I'm sorry to say that one of our researchers was killed last Thursday night and I'm anxious to ascertain his last movements so that we can recover some important research findings he was working on. Although it was nothing to do with our institute, Richard informs me that our late researcher was involved in a campaign against the wind farm on Bargieoch Moor and the proposed Derrydruie development. His name was Colin McCulloch."

Sir Crispin's mood hardened.

"Iew, that little shit – bane of my life. I heard he had been murdered. If I'd my way I'd have throttled him myself. Mind you I never actually met him but my factor Kenny Armstrong tells me he was an obnoxious agitator. He should have . . ."

Before the landowner could continue, his iPhone rang out the tune of 'Land of Hope and Glory'.

"Hellew . . . John . . . Yes . . . Niw . . . Niw . . . Niw – iew shit! . . . I'll leave right away. I should get theh just oftah midnight – say one o' clock. See you at the office first thing . . . Yah, seven o' clock."

He shouted to his housekeeper (she who had opened the front door):

"Mary, pack my bags immediately. I'm oaff to London right now."

He then turned to his two visitors:

"And you two can just piss oaff. And I'd advise you not to employ rabble-rousers in fyootshah."

Richard and the professor retreated from Bargieoch House immediately thereafter to undertake the forty minute drive to Dumfries for their appointment with Minerva Skinner.

MINERVA SKINNER

MINERVA SKINNER lived and worked in Dumfries. She had a small flat in down town Munchies Street. It was to this address, at around seven o' clock, that Professor Macdonald and Brother Richard called. The door was opened by a young woman in her mid-twenties. She had a thin almost emaciated appearance, not improved by long straggly mouse-coloured hair. She wore black jeans and a long brown cardigan over a grey woolly top.

"Good evening Minerva? I phoned last night. I hope we haven't come at an inconvenient time."

"Good evening Professor. Not at all. Please come in."

The visitors were shown into a small but cosy somewhat cluttered sitting room. There were two book cases and on the walls an eclectic collection of prints, photographs, water colours, a couple of small but good quality oils and a poster bearing the text of the Treaty of Arbroath. Minerva was a staunch Scottish Nationalist.

"I hope you don't mind; I have brought Brother Richard Wells along. We are both sorry to disturb your evening, but we just wanted firstly to say how sorry we are about the shocking circumstances of Colin's death."

"Thank you both for coming. I still can't believe what has happened. I just don't understand it. Why . . ?"

Minerva paused and checked a tear, gave a little shudder, brought her emotions under control and continued.

"Colin was here that evening, the night he was . . . The night he died. He was in good form and there was another chap with him. Tom, I think his name was. They had just been at a meeting of the 'Save Derrydruie' committee and the pair of them were full of it. They were sure that the campaign was starting to have an impact. It's funny; I hadn't seen Colin for some time. We had – well – sort of had a row, and then a week ago he turns up again on my door step."

Minerva paused again.

"You know Colin spoke very highly of you Professor Macdonald, and you too Brother Richard. He was so pleased to have been given his position with the Institute and to work in the field that fascinated him. He had quite a difficult time before and, despite what people thought, he lacked confidence. That's why he was often sarcastic and cutting – as a kind of defence. But he was clever and kind hearted and good to me – at least until . . . Oh but you have travelled a long way. Can I offer you tea, coffee – something stronger?"

"Thank you yes tea would be fine."

"Yes, the same for me thanks."

At which Minerva disappeared into her kitchenette, emerging a couple of minutes later with three mugs of tea and a plate of Jaffa Cakes.

As the tea was poured and the two men, not having had an evening meal, munched the Jaffa Cakes, the mood of the company relaxed and the professor spoke.

"We, at the institute, had a high regard for Colin and for the quality and originality of his researches. In fact it will be important to pull his work together into published form. But, if I may ask, how did you and Colin meet ?"

"Ah yes", Minerva's mind was transported back to a happier time, "I'm a Doonhamer* born and bred and a librarian with the local authority. I have an interest in Scottish History. That's how, a couple of years ago, I first

---

* The term *doonhamer* comes from the way that natives of Dumfries over the years have referred to the area when working away from home. The town is often referred to as *doon hame* (down home).

came to know Colin, when he became a regular at the library, by helping him locate some obscure and rarely accessed volumes and documents to aid his studies. Well you know how it is. Our relationship blossomed and Colin stopped over with me at the flat here a few days every week. He used to try out his ideas on me and I enjoyed that and I helped him at one of the Dalmannoch seminars – last February it was."

Encouraged by the way Minerva was opening up, Richard nodded.

"Yes, I remember, we very much appreciated your input and your people skills and, if I may say, your moderating influence on Colin's conduct."

"Ah well", Minerva sighed, "My influence seems to have had its limits".

A tear formed in her eye but again she rallied.

"It was after your spring conference at Dalmannoch that Colin seemed to lose interest in me. After a few weeks I found out that he was having an affair with one of the conference delegates – a floosie called Angela Trevelyan. We had a big row and I saw no more of Colin until a week ago. He told me he was sorry and that it was all over with Angela. He said her husband had found out about the affair and was after his blood. In spite of everything, I was glad to have him back – and then – this . . ."

Richard sympathised:

"I know, it's been a terrible shock to us all. It must have hit you harder than any of us. If there is anything we can do, just say."

Professor Macdonald took the opportunity to lift the mood and asked:

"We called on the police yesterday and on Colin's mother. The police weren't very forthcoming and there was no sign of Colin's laptop at his mother's. You don't have it by any chance do you? It belonged to the institute."

"No, I don't. The police were here too. They asked for it, but of course I didn't have it. They were quite officious. Well the inspector was. I was very upset. They asked a few questions, but didn't stop long when I told them I hadn't seen much of Colin until last week. So no, I'm sorry I don't have the laptop."

"Pity; I'm very keen to look at Colin's notes. They might even give us some clue as to who was responsible for his death. He was scheduled to phone me about his latest findings the day I got word that he had been killed. It was something to do with a mysterious group he had called the 'Elven Knights'. If you do come across his notes, I'd appreciate knowing what you find – I mean about his researches."

Minerva nodded, thought for a moment and then spoke.

"Colin told me quite a lot about his ideas and discoveries. He mentioned the Elven Knights and was very preoccupied about them. From what I recall of what he said, they are some sort of ancient secret order set up to protect some aspect of Galloway's past or heritage or culture or something like that. He was pretty cagy about it all, but he told me that they have a Gaelic name – let me think – yes – it sounded something like 'reejeran shee'".

The professor was astonished,

"This is very interesting. Do you mean this order exists in the present?"

"Well that's what I thought, but maybe I misunderstood. Maybe they are a thing of the past. Colin didn't want to say very much about them."

"Well thank you Minerva, we came to offer our condolences, but you have been very helpful. Now I think we should leave you in peace."

As the two men rose to depart, Richard spoke.

"You mentioned that Colin had a friend with him, Tom I think you said. What was he like ? Did they seem like close friends ?"

"Yes they seemed to get along well. As I said, they were both pretty wound up about the Derrydruie campaign. They stayed for a bite of supper. Colin had a couple of beers but his friend just had tea. He didn't say a lot. He was quite a bit older than Colin and very civil. Apparently he was especially interested in Derrydruie and wanted the site preserved. The police asked who he was, but I had never met him before. I couldn't really give them any more information than I have told you."

With that Richard and the professor gave Minerva their thanks and farewells and headed back to Dalmannoch.

THE MISSING PAGAN

IT WAS JUST AFTER TEN the following morning when fresh news about Thomas Nutter broke. A silver grey Mercedes Benz Dualiner van drew up. It bore the legend 'G Douglas, Plumbing and Heating Engineer, Newton Stewart'. Out of it stepped Gordon Douglas and his ever stunning blond girl friend Suzie Silver. It was Frances who met them at the front door with a:

"Hello, what brings you two here at this hour. Is it about the Gaelic Group meeting tonight ?"

"No, not that", said Suzie, "Holly called to see us yesterday. She said she had told you about Thomas going off without letting anyone know. We called at her place on the way here this morning, but she wasn't in. We wanted to tell her we've just had a message from him."

"Oh good; is he OK? We were all quite concerned." It was Suzie who spoke.

"Well, He's safe, but he's in trouble. Can we go inside? I'd like Brother Richard to know what's going on."

The little group went into the reception room where Richard was alone checking the morning's emails. Suzie reiterated the fact of Thomas's message and continued.

"Thomas phoned Gordon's office this morning just after we opened at half past eight. I took the call. He told me he had gone into hiding because he knew who killed Colin. He made it clear that it wasn't him, but was scared that they were after him too and needed time to work out his next move. He said he couldn't explain on the phone, but on no account to tell the police about his whereabouts or tell anyone else except Holly and yourselves or even to refer to him in any phone conversation. He was worried that the phones of the Pagans or Dalmannoch might be tapped. He said if anyone asked where he was, to say that he had been called away to visit a sick relative. He said he'll make contact again in a few days' time using the code-name 'Screwball', then he hung up.

Frances was flabbergasted.

"What on earth is it all about? In hiding? Code-names? It's just too melodramatic. You don't think he's lost the plot – a brainstorm . . ?"

Richard's take on this extraordinary report was different.

"No, I don't think so. Thomas is level headed – a trained marine, I'm inclined to trust his judgement. In fact his message rather vindicates Ruairidh's and my instinct of holding off informing the police. I'm beginning to sense that there is something not right about this affair."

"Well", Frances volunteered, "Colin getting murdered is certainly not at all right."

"I know, I know, but that's not what I mean. There are aspects of this business that are not as they appear and I can't put my finger on what. Look; we have to keep the lid on this for now. We must not discuss Thomas outside this group – with one exception. We need to bring Professor Macdonald into the frame.

"And," added Frances, "We need to let Holly know Thomas is alright, but no detail and to keep schtum."

On reaching unanimous agreement to this course of action, Suzie and Gordon left to get on with their business activities.

Professor Macdonald had breakfasted early that morning, after which, he had phoned his secretary to deal with some administrative matters that were starting to build up at the Institute in Inverness, not least on the issue of the Institute's finances about which there were some puzzling questions that required resolution. He had then gone into Wigtown to try to track down an elusive monograph in one of the many bookshops in the town. He returned to

Dalmannoch at about quarter to twelve to find Richard hoeing his vegetables.

"Ah, Ruairidh, there you are. I'm glad you have appeared. We've had news about Thomas. Let's go to the kitchen for a chin-wag."

They were joined by Frances who had been busy upstairs. Over coffee, the dramatic tidings brought earlier by Suzie and Gordon were described.

"Well now; that's very interesting – very interesting. It looks as though we were right to hold fire on alerting the police. I think it's time to set out the facts as we understand them. Let's see what they tell us."

After Frances fetched some paper and pens from the reception room, the three of them sat round the kitchen table. Professor Macdonald, with his accustomed academic rigour started the process.

"What do we know? Well we know Colin was killed by stabbing sometime last Thursday evening or early Friday morning and was found at Sweetheart Abbey. Presumably that was where the murder took place. Working back from there; we know that he and Thomas (well we presume it was Thomas) called on Minerva earlier that evening and seemed to be good pals and in good form. So it would appear that their shared interest in preserving Derrydruie from development had overridden their former mutual animosity. But we know too that Colin had antagonised a number of people. Let's make a list."

Each threw in suggestions and amplifications that may be summarised as follows:

1. Duggie Gordon but inconceivable that he would do anything rash
2. Neo-Pagans – although Thomas at least seems to have been exonerated. He has said he wasn't the murderer, but knows who was

72

3. Christian fundamentalists – Colin had written at least two letters to the *Gleaner* criticising their fanaticism
4. Sir Crispin Short – whose multiple sins in Colin's eyes included landowning, wind-farm development, the proposed Derrydruie theme park and activity in the financial sector
5. George Lang – the businessman behind the Derrydruie theme park and an associate of Sir Crispin
6. Councillor Norrie Armstrong – by repute a shady politician in favour of the Derrydruie development
7. Angela Trevelyan's husband who, it was said by Minerva, was 'after Colin's blood'
8. The Elven Knights – whoever they are or were. Did Colin see them as a threat? Minerva rendered their Gaelic name as 'reejeran shee'

Frances read through the list and surmised:

"Derrydruie seems to be a bit of a common theme among quite a few of these – what shall we call them? – suspects?

The others nodded and Richard added:

"Thomas holds the key to the whole thing and until he turns up, I don't think any of us can take things further forward as regards the murder. And I don't suppose the police can either without Thomas. We'll just have to let him emerge in his own time. But perhaps, more importantly for us at Dalmannoch and the Institute, can we uncover Colin's researches? I have been thinking about Colin's Latin list. I should have spotted it immediately. The first line: 'BENEVENTUS VERBEREUS EST' surely refers simply to the wind farm company, Beneventus, as – how could you put it? – to be castigated – in other words Colin's disapproval of that development and desire to see it stopped".

The professor's eyes lit up.

"Well done Richard, let me go up to my room and I'll bring down the paper. Let's see what you make of the rest of it,"

He returned and handed it to Richard who re-examined it.

"Yes, of course, the second line starts to make sense too in the light of our new list of 'suspects', so SICUT CHRISTIANI IMPATIENSES continues extends and compares Colin's disapproval with intolerant Christians, that is I suppose Christian fundamentalists. So he's saying he disapproves equally of wind-farms and Christian fanatics.

Frances, who had been awaiting some astounding revelation, was not greatly impressed.

"This much we already know. What about the next two lines ?"

"Well, let's see: SED MILITES PACIS GALWEDIENSES, CONSERVABUNT SILVA DRUIDAE: the peaceful soldiers . . . or rather, soldiers of peace of Galloway shall save the forest of the druids. The last bit I would have thought must be Derrydruie, so another pointer to that place. But who in heaven's name are the soldiers of peace?"

There was a puzzled silence, a stroking of chins and scratching of heads. It was Frances who piped up.

"Did you say that Minerva called the Elven Knights, 'reejeran shee?' – Well it's obvious surely. Gaelic 'ridirean' – knights and 'sìth'[*] meaning peace, but 'sìth' also means fairy, you know as in our Irish Banshee – fairy woman who foretells death. Don't you see 'ridirean sìth

---

[*] Gaelic sìth pronounced shee

can mean both 'knights of peace' or 'fairy knights, or if you like Elven Knights."

Professor Macdonald slammed the table and couldn't contain his admiration.

"Bingo –you've cracked it ! Frances you are inspired. The 'militii pace' – soldiers of peace or knights of peace were – or are – the Elven Knights. So the last two lines are a kind of antidote to the first two – the Elven Knights of Galloway shall save Derrydruie."

"All very well", Brother Richard pointed out, "but who are the Elven Knights, how are they supposed to save Derrydruie and how does this take us forward?"

The professor advocated looking at the last line: QUAERITE ARAM BARHOBBLE ET INVENIETIS.

"Seek the altar of Barhobble and you shall find it. If there is an answer to your question perhaps we should follow Colin's lead and head for Barhobble."

BARHOBBLE

RICHARD AND RUAIRIDH SET OFF in the professor's old but trusty green Volvo. Along a series of by-roads they passed through Mochram, and headed uphill along an ever narrower lane. As they gained height, a magnificent view of Luce Bay and the Rhins of Galloway opened up. Upwards they continued until they reached a farm steading. There they parked the car and continued on foot, still gaining altitude along a grassy path, round the edge of a wood until they reached the low ruined walls of an ancient building – the medieval chapel of Barhobble.

"Frances and I came up here to have a look last autumn. We were tipped off at the Whithorn Visitor Centre. There's an early cross-slab stone in the centre that came from here. Besides the Christian symbolism, there is also a carved swastika and a Thor's hammer incorporated into a cross. It seems that Christianity and Paganism existed side by side at Barhobble."

The professor nodded in affirmation.

"It's some time since I was up here myself. And of course, I had studied the swastika and hammerhead carvings myself. The archaeology shows several periods of occupation from the 8th to the 14th centuries. I asked Colin to have a good look round to see if he could come up with some new angle. He certainly didn't come back to me with anything, but who knows; he may have been holding back pending a full report."

Richard intervened:

"Let's have a look at the altar. Perhaps we can make sense of Colin's rhyme."

The two men entered the rectangle of low stone work that marked the outline of the little medieval chapel. At the eastern end, raised on a rough dry-stone plinth, lay a large grey recumbent stone slab that had apparently spilt in two – the altar.

"Mm. Nothing unusual that I can see," said the professor. "What can Colin have been driving at – 'QUAERITE ARAM BARHOBBLE ET INVENIETIS – Seek the altar of Barhobble and you shall find it'".

Richard poked around the altar. Between the two portions of the horizontal cap slabs, there was a considerable gap which was partially filled with small jagged stones. Where the gap narrowed towards the back of the altar, Richard noticed that one of the stones was different from the others. It was a small flat round white quartz stone placed on edge in the crevice. Richard pulled it out and examined it.

"Look at this Ruairidh. I found this in the crevice between the caps stones. Look it has an image incised into it. It's another seven pointed star – an Elven star."

Richard handed the white stone to Ruairidh who examined it.

"Mm; this is a particularly symmetrical natural beach pebble. The design is not just scratched on; it's a careful piece of engraving. I wonder who is responsible." The professor added, "Whoever it was, I suppose this stone must be what Colin was alluding to in his list. I guess we should take it with us back to Dalmannoch. I can't see anything else here that can help us, but perhaps we should take another look to see if anything strikes us."

The two men regarded the site and walked around its perimeter and then again inspected the interior of what remained of the old chapel, but to little avail. After a time Richard concluded:

"This is a fascinating place right enough, especially for me as a former monk, but I think that's it for now. I doubt if we'll find anything more here. Colin's list referred specifically to the altar and that's where we found our only clue – whatever it's supposed to tell us."

"You're right", concurred the professor, "Let's head back to Dalmannoch".

With that, Ruairidh handed the white incised stone back to Richard and the pair made their way back down the grassy path towards the car.

As they walked, Ruairidh admired the view from this high vantage point, but Richard had been deep in thought.

"I was just thinking about the places mentioned in Colin's list. When we went to Derrydruie, we found a piece of cloth bearing an Elven star, and now at Barhobble we find another Elven star carved into a stone – a white stone. That can't be a coincidence. I just wonder if the star may somehow be a common link between the different elements in the list." He pondered further: "Of course, our good friends in the Wigtown Wicca Coven use the Elven star surrounded by a circle as their symbol, but I remember, a year ago when we first got access to the interior of our chapel at Dalmannoch, you pointed out the Elven star to me. You told me it had magical or sacred significance."

"Well yes it does," the professor confirmed.

"The Elven star, or Faerie star represents the seven stars of the Pleiades, also known as the Seven Sisters after the daughters of Atlas & Pleione. In Greek mythology, Orion the hunter fell in love with the sisters and their mother. He chased them for seven years trying to woo them. In the end, Zeus intervened and turned the seven sisters into doves to help them escape Orion's attention. The doves flew into the heavens to become the constellation Pleiades, which means 'the doves'. The Pleiades have been revered ever since as the centre of the Universe, the seat of immortality and the home of the Divine. So the Faerie Star is believed to symbolise the gateway between the mortal human realm and the Otherworld.

But it's the seven points that are particularly noteworthy. Seven is a sacred number in many magical traditions; a lucky prime number, a happy number and a safe number. Hence we have the seven pillars of wisdom, seven days of Creation, the seven days of the week and the seven colours of the rainbow the seven virtues and the seven deadly sins and so on.

The other feature of the Elven star is that it is made up of a single interlaced strand, which I suppose could be taken to represent continuity and a binding together.

However, all that being so, where does it get us?"

"Beats me", admitted Brother Richard.

EVENING REVELATIONS

T HAT EVENING, being a Wednesday, the members
of the Galloway Gaelic Group (in Gaelic 'Grunnan
Gàidhlig Ghallghaidhealaibh' or GGG for short)
assembled in Dalmannoch's common room for their
weekly class.

The group had grown out of a mutual interest in the
Celtic heritage of Galloway and especially in learning and
using the Gaelic language, which had been prevalent in
Galloway in times past. Whilst still spoken and promoted
in the Scottish Highlands and Islands and some other parts
of Scotland, Gaelic had died out in Galloway around the
beginning of the 18th century.

The first to arrive was Duggie Gordon with his
wife Trish. They had married in the spring. Inevitably as an
accountant, Duggie was the group secretary and treasurer
and always prompt to collect the "subs".

Richard opened the door and Frances, who by dint
of her own native Irish Gaelic had quickly reached a good
workable fluency in the Scottish form of the language,
welcomed them:

"Feasgar math dhaimh. Thigibh a steach agus
fàilte".[1]

"Tapadh leibh agus ciamar a tha sibh a nochd?"[2]
was the response.

And so such pleasantries continued as by quick succession
others arrived: Iain Stewart carrying a guitar case in the
off-chance hope of a session; a group of new members; a
middle aged couple from Gatehouse of Fleet, Sebastian

---

[1] Pronounced Feskar mah ghive. Heekiv ashtshach agus faal-tshi (ch as
in Scottish loch), meaning: Good evening to you. Come in and
welcome.

[2] Pronounced Tapa live agus Kimir a ha shiv a nochk? Meaning:
Thanks and how are you tonight?

Craig and his wife Ailsa, a young well-built red-haired man Cuthbert (or Cuddie) McGrotty from Kirkowan, who had *en route* collected Peggy McKie, a raven haired farmer's daughter in her early thirties, from near Sorbie. Next came group stalwarts: silver haired, moustachioed and affable Ronald Radcliff with his two lady friends, Ellen Crawford and Sophie Hamilton, in tow. Just behind them the Mercedes van of Gordon Douglas and Suzie Silver arrived followed a minute later by the Ford Focus of musicians Angus and Fiona Martin.

The creation of the group about eighteen months before had been the initiative of Suzie Silver who had persuaded her boy-friend Gordon Douglas and their accountant friend Duggie Gordon to place an advert in the *Galloway Gleaner* seeking to flush out others interested in the heritage of Galloway and especially in learning Gaelic. In the event about a dozen others had responded. These formed the core of the group and while a few had dropped off at an early date, a couple of others (the Martins) had joined subsequently. Through his accountancy connections, Duggie had identified the Reverend Donald Angus MacLeod, a Gaelic speaking Church of Scotland minister, originally from Skye and persuaded him to become their tutor. The bearded clergyman had proven to be a valuable find – an accomplished piper and to quote Duggie:

"He's very broad minded – for a minister."

At first the group had met on sequential weeks in members' houses, then in a hotel in Newton Stewart and eventually and most satisfactorily, since the previous summer, at Dalmannoch, even before it had become fully operational. In fact the GGG members had been willing helpers in the renovation of the building from its previous dilapidated condition.

In those early days of the joint venture between the GGG and Brother Richard, Duggie had explained that to

aid their learning the group used the 'Ùlpan' method, a
language immersion scheme that had originated in Israel,
when faced with a massive influx of refugee immigrants
soon after the creation of that state in 1948. The method
was designed to teach adults basic Hebrew language skills
of conversation, writing and comprehension and has since
been adapted and adopted by other nations attempting to
revive their own minority or lost languages. And so, among
others, the Ùlpan model has been employed to teach Welsh
in Wales, Sami in Norway and of course Gaelic in Scotland.

On this particular Wednesday evening, the
Reverend Donald Angus was later than usual in arriving
and when he did, he was accompanied by another
newcomer to the group. She was one Agnes Morrison, a
fluent native Gaelic speaker, originally from Ness on the
Island of Lewis, now a primary teacher in Stranraer and
living in Glenluce. She had been recruited by Donald
Angus to provide an additional tuition resource. To cater
for the new members, the group was split into two sets. The
more advanced students were taken by the minister to the
common room, while the beginners or less fluent took their
places round the library table, under the wing of Agnes.

And so the business of Gaelic drills and converstion
practice continued for about an hour and a half. After that a
less formal social part of the evening commenced in the
common room, the venue for many a cèilidh. The main
interest that evening was quizzing Agnes about herself and
the Isle of Lewis. Soon the Gaelic activists were
enthusiastically joining in the chorus of a song that Agnes
Morrison had been teaching them. It was about Agnes's
native Isle of Lewis and was called *Eilean beag donn a'
chuain* – the little brown island of the sea – a lovely song,
although it was noted by the, at times pedantic Duggie, that
at over two thousand square kilometres, Lewis with Harris

is the third largest island of the British Isles after Great Britain itself and Ireland.

Although of somewhat serious demeanour, Agnes's patient approach and melodic singing voice had already endeared her to the group.

While this informal session was in progress Brother Richard ushered the Reverend Donald Angus into the reception room, which served as an office. As has been noted, notwithstanding their differing spiritual paths; Richard a Roman Catholic ex-monk and Donald Angus a Presbyterian, the pair were firm friends and shared a huge mutual respect.

Shutting the door behind him, Richard spoke:

"I was hoping to sound you out about a curious thing – well a couple of things that occurred over the last few days."

"I'm all ears, fire away my friend."

Richard produced the note that had been delivered to Dalmannoch the previous Friday and passed it over to the minister.

Donald Angus read it aloud.

"As righteousness tendeth to life: So he that pursueth evil pursueth it to his own death.

Mm Proverbs eleven: nineteen from the King James Bible, if I'm not mistaken. The verse that follows, goes:

They that are of a forward heart are abomination to the Lord: but such as are upright in their way are his delight."

Richard clapped his hands.

"I'm impressed by your Old Testament knowledge, but then you are a minister – and a Presbyterian to boot. I had managed to track down the quotation myself. The thing is; this was sent to me anonymously out of the blue. Then Ruairidh Macdonald and I heard the same quotation a few days later spouted from a street preacher in Dumfries. What makes it odder is that the preacher looked expressly at me as he said it – as though he recognised me. He harangued the crowd about failing churches and preachers and depraved unbelievers and sinners. He then referred to what he called the Elect of the Revelation commanding repentance and threatening hell.

The other thing that niggles me is that the note was delivered the day immediately following the murder of Colin McCulloch – you know our researcher here. Maybe there's nothing in that, except that Colin was an outspoken critic of fundamentalist Christians and this chap in Dumfries certainly seemed to be pretty fundamentalist in his approach.

Have you heard of this Elect of the Revelation?"

"Oh, indeed I have," confirmed Donald Angus. "It is a pretty hard line group – small in number but strident in their 'approach' to use your word. Their leader is a man called Pastor Erskine Mutch. He's a Zealot with a capital 'Z'. He's originally from somewhere in Northern Ireland and from what I heard; he was encouraged to leave his native heath about a year ago – some financial irregularity. So he set up shop in Scotland.

"So where is his church?" Richard wondered.

"Well that's the thing," Donald Angus continued. "He doesn't seem to have a centre of operations as such. He has a scattering of adherents from all over Scotland, but mostly in the south-west – Ayrshire, Galloway, Dumfries-shire. It seems they meet at conventicles, often in the open-air in the manner of the old Covenanters.

"Ah yes", said Richard, "I have been reading about the Covenanters and the Killing Times in the 17th century, when rebel ministers refused to recognise the restored bishops and how they preached to their congregations at secret illegal open-air meetings in the countryside even although it was a capital offence to attend such meetings.

They must have been resolute in their beliefs and very brave in the face of the terrible oppression they suffered. What is so sad is the unyielding intolerance on both sides of the divide. Thank God we live in a more tolerant age now."

"Amen to that Richard. Unfortunately, from what I have heard, the Elect of the Revelation do not share your view on tolerance. They are pretty secretive about their activities, but one of my elders, Willie Christie, managed to evangel himself along to a conventicle that was held a week ago up in the Glenkens to get a flavour. There weren't that many of them – about forty or fifty at the most, but he was horrified. There was scant love and forgiveness and much hatred of anyone and anything that was not in strict accordance with their narrow and extreme interpretation of Scripture. In fact Willie told me that Dalmannoch had been held up as, to quote his and Pastor Erskine Mutch's words, 'a den of Paganism, Popery, Prelacy, Malignancy and Sectarianism and an abomination to the Lord'. I wouldn't have mentioned it were it not for what you have just told me about the note and your experience at Dumfries. Anyway, I've asked Willie to keep in contact with them just to see what they're up to."

Richard thought for a minute then spoke:

"Well it seems clear that this bunch of extremists has Dalmannoch and its works in their sights, but surely they wouldn't go to the length of murder – would they?

MORNING DISCUSSIONS

PROFESSOR RUAIRIDH MACDONALD had, since
its inception, been a strong supporter of the
Galloway Gaelic Group, but he had other business
that Wednesday evening. After a telephone conversation
with his wife, he had gone out to visit an academic friend
and collaborator. He had, therefore, not been present for the
Gaelic group's activities. It was late by the time he returned
to Dalmannoch. The Galloway Gaelic group had long
departed and gone their separate ways. Sleep beckoned and
he retired straight away to his room.

Next morning over breakfast in the kitchen Richard
told the professor about his chat with the Reverend
MacLeod and his portrayal of the Elect of the Reformation
as extreme and intolerant fundamentalists who seemed to
'have it in for' Dalmannoch.

Frances was the first to react:

"Sure by the sound of it they're hardly overflowing
with Christian charity."

There was nodding consent all round.

Ruairidh, in professorial mode, expounded:

"Of course schisms and dissent from the
mainstream are nothing new in Scottish religious life. We
Scots can be a disputatious bunch, especially when it
comes to matters of principle. The church has a long
history of secessions followed by breakaways from the
secessionists followed by re-groupings. As often as not,
when the original reason for a split has been resolved or
largely forgotten, however important it may have been at
the time, and amalgamation has been proposed, one faction
would favour the merger while another would remain "out".
They're still at it today within the Free Church and within
the Church of Scotland itself.

But, Frances is right; this Elect of the Revelation crowd are something else by the sound of it. I'm just wondering, from what you tell me about the note you got the day after Colin was murdered; and then the guy we heard shooting his mouth off in Dumfries and what Donald Angus told you about their apparent hatred of Dalmannoch . . . Well I'm just wondering if one of Pastor Erskine Mutch's flock might have been responsible for Colin's death. I mean you do hear of deranged religious fanatics killing people out of some kind of misplaced notion of retribution."

"I must confess; the same thought had crossed my own mind," Richard admitted. "I was wondering if we should ring the police, or are we jumping to conclusions?

"We're not jumping to conclusions – merely raising a suspicion. Remember that Inspector Huxtable mentioned the possibility of some form of ritualistic killing and he did say to let him know if we came up with anything that might help their enquiries."

Richard nodded: "True, true. OK, it would be best Ruairidh if you rang them, since it was you the police contacted in the first place. But no mention of Thomas Nutter. I'm clear in my mind that he is not the murderer and we must respect his wishes about not contacting the police about his movements. We will find out more when he re-appears."

"Fine. I'll call Inspector Huxtable when we have finished breakfast."

In the meantime Frances was ploughing through that morning's *Daily Caledonian*.

"It looks as though there may have been another murder. They've found the body of a young girl washed up yesterday evening on the shore near Southerness. It says here she had been missing from the Craigdoune Childrens' Home in Dumfries since last Thursday night and that there are signs of foul play but it doesn't give any more detail. Poor wee lassie. She was only fourteen."

There was general assent that the loss of such a young life in evil circumstances was a shameful indictment on modern society.

And so it was, after breakfast that, with Richard at his side, Professor Ruairidh Alasdair Macdonald repaired to the reception room and put through a call to the Dumfries police.

"Ah, good morning. Would you put me through to Inspector Huxtable please . . . Professor Ruairidh Macdonald from the MacPhedran Institute of Celtic Studies. Inspector Huxtable knows who I am . . . Yes Macdonald . . . Thank you . . . Ah, yes good morning Inspector Huxtable. You will recall, when Brother Richard Wells and I met with you on Monday, you asked us to let you know if we had any further information that might help you about the matter of our researcher Colin McCulloch's death . . . Well yes. I'm not sure how helpful this is, but . . ."

The professor then described the chain of events that the pair had discussed over breakfast, which he concluded with:

"So really what I am saying is that the timing of these events and my researcher's death may be coincidence, but Brother Richard and I felt we should at least inform you in case there was some connection."

The professor was somewhat surprised at the inspector's reaction. This he conveyed to Richard when the call was finished.

"Well, that man! I didn't much take to him when we saw him in Dumfries and my opinion of him hasn't improved. Did I get thanks for my call? Not in the slightest. He told me he was well aware of the Elect of the Revelation, that they were devout Christians and the notion that they could be involved with murder was unthinkable. He even suggested that perhaps we should look closer to home for a motive and a suspect, or suspects.

How that man rose to become an inspector I do not know."

HECTOR ARRIVES

IT WAS IN THE LATE AFTERNOON of the same day that Hector Woodrow Douglas arrived at Dalmannoch. Hector was a pivotal figure in the re-birth of Dalmannoch as a functioning enterprise. Although for many years domiciled in Canada, he was chief of the Green Douglases, a minor sept of the Douglas Clan. It had in fact been his great grandfather, Sir Joseph Douglas, a noted antiquarian, who had founded Dalmannoch more than a century earlier.

Hector maintained a controlling interest in Woodrow Douglas Logistics, a profitable freight forwarding business in British Columbia, with a particular involvement in the burgeoning China and Far-East trade. Nowadays he left much of the day-to-day running of the business to his son James. This allowed Hector to devote time and energy to other interests. Indeed, such was his interest in his family heritage that he was a major financial contributor to, and chairman of, the new Dalmannoch Foundation and he endeavoured to make periodic visits to Scotland, while basing himself at the comfortable apartment set aside for him.

Richard was alerted to Hector's arrival by the engine noise of a dusty grey Land Rover discovery. The distinguished Hector emerged wearing a dark business suit, pale blue shirt and Douglas tartan tie. As Richard stood at the open front door he was greeted by an outstretched hand and man-hug.

"Richard; you son of a gun. You look in rude good heath. How are you and your good lady?"

"Oh, fine, fine; and how are you? You're looking, what can I say – very dapper yourself. Come in. Come in."

On hearing the exchange, Frances appeared.

"Hector. You're here at last. How lovely to see you."

The Chief of the Green Douglases, with his relaxed old-fashioned, North American charm, beheld Frances and kissing her on both cheeks declared:

"Frances! You look more beautiful than ever. How do you do it?"

"Away with you Hector, It's an Irishman you should be with all that Blarney. Sure life with Richard here at Dalmannoch is better than a tonic. But, hey, you'll be tired after your travels. Let's get your luggage inside. Your apartment's ready and I'll make you a coffee. Have you eaten?"

"A coffee would be grand, thanks Frances. I've just spent three days in London and Southampton with logistics folk, financiers, shipping companies, cargo owners, agents, lawyers and officials and glad to be here at last to get into something more agreeable. For now I'll just go upstairs, settle in and have a bit of shut-eye, then maybe we can have a powwow over dinner."

With that Richard helped Hector transfer luggage from car to apartment whereat the Canadian made himself at home in his comfortable quarters while Richard withdrew to his chores.

In anticipation of dinner, Richard, Frances and Ruairidh had already foregathered in Dalmannoch's cosy kitchen. Ruairidh had spent much of the day 'out' following his academic pursuits. It was half past six by the time Hector reappeared. He had changed into more informal polo shirt, lightweight jumper, slacks and loafers, undoubtedly from some quality source.

"Boy, I feel much the better of a snooze and a shower. The last few days have been quite demanding and I'm not quite so young as I used to be. Pretty successful though, so I think I deserve a change of scene and a bit of recreation. I have to say, the train service over here beats anything in Canada or the States. I left Euston at half past nine and was at Carlisle by quarter to twelve. James, my cousin met me there and drove me to his place. Hilda, his wife made me a snack lunch. James lent me his old four-by-four and here I am.

Ruairidh, you may be interested to come up with me some time to my cousin's place. James and Hilda are Douglases like me. They run Glenshillan. It's a nice little sporting estate about three quarters of an hour from here. Richard and Frances have been there. We could perhaps all go once we get the trustees meeting out of the way."

"I'd love that, although I'm not much of a shot – more of a fisherman, but after our meeting, I'll need to get back to Inverness for a few days."

There was general agreement that once Ruairidh returned from Inverness, a visit to Glenshillan would be arranged.

By this point in the conversation the meal was ready and duly served – smoked salmon starter, a main course of roast lamb with potatoes and vegetables fresh from Richard's vegetable garden followed by fresh fruit salad.

Over the meal Hector, who had already heard of the death of Colin McCulloch, was brought up to date regarding much of the previous week's events. The matter of Thomas Nutter's disappearance was avoided, however.

"Gee whiz! What a weird turn of events. And the police haven't arrested anyone?"

Richard confirmed that, unless some very recent progress had been made on that front, there had been no arrest, nor, so far as he and others round the table knew, suspects even, other than a vague suggestion by Inspector Huxtable of some ritualistic motive.

"You say that Colin had got up quite a number of people's noses, but the police don't seem to be biting."

Ruairidh nodded and added:

"In the last few days we have been following up a few clues ourselves, but it hasn't got us very far. One of the tragedies of the affair is that Colin was working on some ground breaking research on the juxtaposition of Paganism and Christianity here in Galloway and was scheduled to tell me all about it on the day after he was murdered. The thing is, we can't track down his computer, so I don't even have access to his notes. There were a few CDs in his room but I checked them out and they are all music – nothing that would help us. One thing he mentioned to me, though, was a revelation about some group called the Elven Knights.

Hector listened impassively as Ruairidh outlined his frustration about the inaccessibility of Colin's researches. The professor continued:

"One clue he did leave was a handwritten sort of verse in Latin that we more or less deciphered."

Richard rose from the table, opened a kitchen drawer, extracted the document and handed it to Hector. The latter scrutinised it, handed it back and admitted:

"I ain't much of a Latin buff these days I'm afraid. Did it at school but a bit rusty now. You'll need to fill me in?"

Richard volunteered to do so:

"Well the first two lines seem to be a sort of invective against firstly a proposed wind farm development on Bargieoch Moor, which is on land owned by a Sir Crispin Short, and secondly against what we interpret as Christian fundamentalists and probably a group called the Elect of the Revelation who seem to have a particular dislike of Dalmannoch – thanks probably to Colin.

The next two lines can be translated as 'the soldiers of peace of Galloway shall save the forest of the druids'. We think the forest of the druids refers to a place called Derrydruie where the same Sir Crispin and others propose to develop a leisure theme-park. Like the wind-farm and the fundamentalists, Colin was actively opposed to the despoliation of Derrydruie, it being an ancient sacred site.

The soldiers of peace reference puzzled us. Then we recalled that when we had asked Colin's girlfriend Minerva if she had heard of the Elven Knights, she confirmed that Colin had mentioned them as some sort of ancient secret order set up to protect some aspect of Galloway's heritage and that they had a Gaelic name she related as 'reejeran shee'. It was Frances who put two and two together by pointing out that the Gaelic word 'sith' can mean either 'peace' or 'faerie' hence Ridirean Sìth can mean soldiers or knights of peace or faerie or Elven knights.

The last line goes – 'Seek the altar of Barhobble and you shall find it'. So yesterday, Ruairidh and I went to the old ruined chapel at Barhobble to have a look around. We came away none the wiser except that we found this." Richard rose again and in the same drawer extracted the round white stone inscribed with a seven pointed Elven Star. He handed it to Hector.

Hector inspected the stone. His expression was difficult to read as he seemed to weigh up deep thoughts. The others watched, curious at Hector's apparent change in mood. Then Hector spoke:

"Well you guys have certainly been busy. You have figured out mysteries that have long remained hidden."

This statement came as something of a surprise to the rest of the group who felt that they had made little progress in understanding what was behind Colin's death, let alone uncovering ancient mysteries.

Ruairidh responded.

"I don't quite understand Hector. What mysteries have we uncovered? Can you tell us something about the Elven Knights and the significance of this stone?"

Hector Woodrow-Douglas frowned, looked long and hard at each of them in turn. He considered carefully before speaking.

"The Elven Knights? I *can* tell you about the Elven Knights – but – before I do, I must have your absolute assurance that what I say will be kept in the very strictest confidence.

Again he looked at each of them. One by one – Richard – Frances – Ruairidh – they nodded in affirmation.

"You must each swear on the Bible that, unless sanctioned by me, you will never ever divulge what I am about to reveal you."

Brother Richard left the room for a few seconds and returned with a large black Bible upon which each pledged on oath to keep Hector's secret.

A TEMPLAR'S LEGACY

ECTOR WOODROW-DOUGLAS turned his head to look out of the kitchen window, as if seeking inspiration and checking that no one else was around. He paused for a moment to gather his thoughts and then spoke.

"We must go back to the year 1138. In that year David I, King of Scots launched an invasion of northern England. Although Galloway was then a kingdom independent of both Scotland and England, Fergus, King of Galloway had been persuaded to provide men in support of David's campaign. In the course of hostilities the Scots and Gallovidians wrought terror, destruction and havoc against the country folk of the invaded territory. Worse; atrocities against women and children were so shocking that Archbishop Thurstan of York was moved to lead a Northumbrian force to confront the invaders. In the subsequent battle at Cowton Moor, near Northallerton, the Northumbrians set up a mast on a wagon displaying banners of the saints Wilfred of Ripon, John of Beverly and St Peter of York. The Gallovidians were fierce and dauntless fighters, but, uncharacteristically, they broke ranks and fled the field. You see, the Scots had their own ecclesiastical structure, but Thurstan was the Gallovidians own archbishop and, at that time, they revered the same saints as the Northumbrians.

This episode was known thereafter as the Battle of the Standard which was to leave a dark stain on the reputation of Galloway that grew with the telling.

By this time Fergus had already ruled Galloway successfully for some twenty years. He was politically astute and his kingdom was prosperous, but he was sensitive to accusations by outsiders of Gallovidian barbarity. As an antidote to this slight, and no doubt to mollify Bishop Thrustan, he saw patronage of the church as a means of demonstrating that Galloway was a progressive and civilised kingdom. Ten years before the Battle of the Standard, Fergus had revived the ancient bishopric of Whithorn under the tutelage of the archbishopric of York. In the years that followed the battle, Fergus sponsored the erection of Dundrennan Abbey and a new cathedral at Whithorn. He established a community of cannons at Soulseat and granted the lands of Galtway to the Knights Hospitaller."

Hector paused and Ruairidh took the opportunity to speak:

"There is nothing secret about all this, Hector. It's to be found in the history text books. In fact Professor Dan Osmond gave Fergus King of Galloway a good airing in our second Dalmannoch seminar. I admit, though, that you summarise these events very well, but the thing is: where do the Elven Knights come in?"

"Ah ha; I'm coming to that." Hector recommenced his monologue. "What I am about to tell does not figure in any text book and is most certainly strictly only for the ears of those assembled here. You see, while all this was going on, Fergus was approached by a man called Arthur de Nouant who had served as a Knight Templar in the Holy Land. The year was probably 1140 or 1141. It is not clear who Arthur was, but he is thought to have been descended from one of the old Welsh Galloway families, and was possibly a cousin of Fergus. Arthur had seen numerous atrocities committed by the Crusaders in the Holy Land and urged Fergus to establish a secret order dedicated to the peaceful well-being of Fergus's realm.

Fergus acceded to this proposal, and at Derrydruie, in a secret ceremony, the *Militii Pace Galwediae* or Order of the Galloway Knights of Peace, known in the Gaelic vernacular as Ridirean Sìth, was inaugurated. At the holy well, King Fergus himself washed the hands and feet of each of the seven men who were to make up the order. Each in turn swore an oath of commitment to maintaining the traditions and security of the realm of Galloway and to each other. On acceptance to the order, each Knight was given a green mantle emblazoned with a silver interlaced seven pointed star. With Arthur as their Grand Master, the Knights were answerable to Fergus himself but were given the power to select their own successors. Their strategic role was to work under cover to resist oppression while encouraging tolerance and understanding.

Those were violent times of course and it was no easy task to encourage peace among ambitious and ruthless magnates. As Fergus aged, his sons Uchtred and Gilbert squabbled for their father's patrimony. Then when Malcolm IV King of Scots, the successor of David, was away in France the Galovidians invaded Desnes Cro, a Scottish territory between the rivers Nith and Urr. When Malcolm returned from France, he mounted a punitive expedition to Galloway. Fergus and his sons were crushed. The Knights of Peace together with their allies, the Scottish Knights Templar based in their preceptory at Balantrodach in Midlothian, brokered favourable peace terms under which Uchtred was given title to Desnes Cro and the land east of the river Cree while Gilbert ruled the western districts and Carrick, but both now under the overlorship of the King of Scots. As you will know, Fergus retired to Holyrood Abbey where he died peacefully the following year and so ended the independent Kingdom of Galloway.

Uchtred started feudalising his territory by introducing Anglo-Norman barons while Gilbert ruled in the old Gaelic way. Their fraternal enmity accelerated. During a period of Anglo-Scottish strife Gilbert's son Malcolm captured Uchtred, put out his eyes and tongue and castrated him after which he died. Thereafter Gilbert ruled all Galloway until his own death in 1185. Then the tables were turned. Uchtred's son Roland was able to reclaim his father's lands then to take Gilbert's territory in western Galloway, thereafter assuming the Lordship of Galloway. He was succeeded by his son Alan, greatest of the native Lords of Galloway, whose fleet of galleys roamed the Irish Sea and western seaboard in trade and warfare.

On Alan's death in 1234, with no legitimate male heir, his patrimony was divided among his three daughters who had all married Anglo-Norman barons. This was abhorrent to the Community of Galloway and to the Knights of Peace who supported the concept of a single Lordship under the rule of Alan's illegitimate son Thomas. The subsequent rebellion was crushed by Alexander II, King of Scots, and the tripartite division was upheld. When the eldest sister Christina died without issue, her share was divided between the remaining two – Elena and Dervorgilla. Of the two, Devorgilla, was to become a legend for her generosity and gentility. She had married John Balliol and bore four sons and four daughters to him. Never before or since had the Knights of Peace a happier collaboration than with Lady Devorgilla of Galloway.

The good times ended dramatically when Alexander III, King of Scots, fell to his death in 1286. In the course of the disputed succession and with Edward of England's connivance, Dervorgilla's son John Balliol became King of Scots; but, as a puppet of Edward, this 'Toom Tabbard' did not reign for long. By 1296 Edward had taken over Scotland and, within a year, rebellion broke out and so commenced the long Wars of Scottish Independence.

In 1306 Robert Bruce was crowned King of Scots, after slaying the Red Comyn at Greyfriers Kirk in Dumfries. Bruce was excommunicated and the fat was in the fire so to speak. Much of Galloway remained loyal to the Balliol cause and for the first time the Order of the Galloway

Knights of Peace was bitterly divided. Some supported Bruce as a saviour; others were opposed.

But it was events in continental Europe that began to refocus the Knights' course of action. At dawn on Friday 13th October 1307, 'Black Friday', many French Knights Templar, including their Grand Master Jacques de Molay, were arrested on the orders of King Philip IV of France on trumped up charges of heresy, sodomy, blasphemy and denying Christ. Confessions were extracted under torture. Reluctantly, under pressure from Philip, Pope Clement V issued the bull *Pastoralis Praeeminentiae*, ordering the arrest of all Templars in Europe. Hearings dragged on for a number of years but in the end the order was dissolved and Jacques de Molay, protesting his and his order's innocence was burnt at the stake in Paris on the 18th of March 1314.

Many French Templars, however, escaped with their treasure. Of their number, a group sailed, via the west of Ireland, to the one place where the pope's decree did not apply – the excommunicate Kingdom of the Scots. The Templars were of course Europe's most accomplished military tacticians and Bruce welcomed them with open arms to aid his long struggle against the English for Scottish independence. Three of the Knights of Peace threw their lot in with the Templars and with two of Bruce's most loyal comrades in arms. One of these was Henry St. Clair of Rosslyn who had close links with the Templars. The other was my ancestor James Douglas, who we also know, depending on your point of view, as either 'Good Sir James' or 'Black Douglas', who had been dispossessed by Edward. With their help Bruce secured Galloway in 1313. As history records, Bruce's final triumph came at Bannockburn in midsummer 1314.

From that time onwards the Knights of Peace, vowed never again to become embroiled in war or in politics or in public life, but to help those who were unjustly treated by the law and as such they seemed to disappear from view and entered folklore as the Elven Knights."

SECRETS SHARED

THE OTHERS HAD LISTENED in wrapped silence to Hector Woodrow-Douglas as he had described these events of olden times. Hector interrupted his discourse to recharge his glass with wine.

Ruairidh, as a historian, had been following the thread of Hector's account with close interest.

"This is fascinating stuff Hector. I was of course aware of the momentous historical events you have described, but completely unaware of the role of these Knights of Peace in shaping them. But," he paused, "I still don't see the need for secrecy. This all happened a very long time ago. Surely it would be of academic and indeed general interest for the story of the Elven Knights to be more widely known."

Hector smiled and held up his hand as a gesture to stop Ruairidh.

"Yes. I understand exactly why you, as an academic, would want to disseminate such information, but I haven't finished my tale yet. Then you will understand the need for secrecy – at least for the present.

To continue just a little more; as I said the Elven Knights had entered folklore and were believed to be imbued with supernatural, or as time passed, with sinister powers. Many tales were told of their exploits, such as that of Lady Isobel and the Elf Knight, whereby the knight woos the lady with music causing the lady to profess love to him:

> 'If I had yon horn that I hear blawing,
> And you elf-knight to sleep in my bosom.'

There were other stories of abduction to the faerie world and such like."

At this point Frances interceded:

"This is weird. Holly Garden told us just such a story about how a young Lord Douglas was enchanted by an Elfin Knight into a magic circle to his almost certain undoing, to be rescued in the end by his friend Lord St. Clair."

"Exactly", confirmed Hector. "I know that story, and you will observe the names of the two main characters, Lords Douglas and St. Clair, the very families with which the Knights of Peace were associated at the time of the Wars of Independence. The stories and ballads associated with the Elven Knights had their equivalents in the Gaelic tradition of the *Daoine Sìth* or Faerie People or more euphemistically – the Little Folk.

By the time of the Reformation and its aftermath, stories of Elven folk came to be dismissed as either for the amusement of children or as objectionable superstition. All the while, however, the Order of the Galloway Knights of Peace, whose members never numbered more than seven, continued in existence – at times quite actively and at other times almost moribund, but always quietly, behind the scenes so to speak. In some ways the folk tales served as a useful cover for the Order's activities. Two sites, because of their relative seclusion, were of importance to the Knights for meetings and ceremonial purposes. These were Derrydruie and Barhobble.

On one occasion when King James IV was on pilgrimage to St Ninian's shrine at Whithorn, another of my ancestors, Reginald Douglas, who was a member of the Order, saved the king from assassins. King James made his escape in the back of a cart, covered with Reginald's green mantle. For this act, Reginald was granted land in the Machars and that is how our branch of the clan came to be known as the Green Douglases.

During the religious conflicts of the 17th century, the Knights were particularly active. Catholics were disinherited; Covenanters were hunted down tortured and killed; Episcopalians were reviled and unyielding fanatical hatred between one group of adherents and the others haunted the land. Yet, in that poisonous environment, many were the fugitives that were hidden and led to safety by the Knights regardless of their religious belief. Then there were the trials and execution of women, and sometimes men for witchcraft. Confessions by these unfortunates of pacts with the Devil or harming neighbours by maleficent witchcraft were commonly extracted by torture and sleep deprivation. Where they could, the Knights intervened to disprove wrongful accusations although I fear the success rate was not high.

You see, while individually the Knights outwardly went along with the religious conventions of the time, they equally, but secretly respected the old religion."

At this point Richard broke in:

"By old religion, do you mean Catholicism?"

"Not exactly," Hector continued, "I mean, they had a broad view of spirituality and ritual, including the forces of the natural and human world as interpreted by our Pagan predecessors.

Which brings me to another of my ancestors – my great grandfather Sir Joseph Douglas. As I have told you before Richard, he was interested in ancient beliefs and especially in the Celtic world. When he married my great grandmother, Lady Mary Blundell, a wealthy English heiress and a Catholic, he built and endowed Dalmannoch in recognition of her religious affiliation. As you know Dalmannoch was established by him as both a place of Catholic retreat, but also as a place that recognised and celebrated the other aspects of Galloway's rich and ancient spiritual and cultural heritage. What I have not told you is that Sir Joseph was the Grand Master of the Order of the Galloway Knights of Peace, or the Elven Knights as they had come to call themselves. Not only that, but he had created the Chapel here to function both as a Catholic chapel and secretly as the preceptory for the Order – its HQ in other words."

"Wow! Now I'm beginning to understand," Ruairidh exclaimed. "When Richard and I got into the chapel for the first time a year ago, we were bowled over by richness of the decoration and the amalgam of Catholic, Celtic and Pagan symbolism. And now you're telling us that, as recently as a century or so ago, the Elven Knights were still functioning as a going concern."

"Yes I am, and not only that, I can tell you that the Order continues to function to this day. As you are jointly and severally sworn to secrecy . . ."

Hector made eye contact with Richard, Ruairidh and Frances in turn and each nodded in acknowledgement

"I can also tell you that I, myself have been a Knight of the order for quite a number of years, as was Alexander Agnew, who was so brutally murdered a year ago."

There were gasps of incredulity and an exchange of glances around the kitchen table among the others of the small gathering.

Frances was the first to speak:

"My God Hector, you're a dark horse, so you are. I'm flabbergasted. I would never have guessed in a hundred years that you were involved in – well – I don't know what to say – a secret society."

"The Order functions in secret and has done for centuries Frances, because that is the best way of ensuring the effectiveness of our mission which is to protect Galloway's rich and ancient spiritual and cultural heritage and to help those who are unjustly treated by the law.

Richard's mind had been racing ahead.

"Now I can see why you and Alexander Agnew were so keen to see Dalmannoch saved from the hands of developers and brought under the control of a new foundation – a structure that unknown to us would serve the ends of the Elven Knights. I have to say I feel a bit – well – misled."

"Please don't feel that Richard, It's true that, because of the Order's strict vow of secrecy, I couldn't reveal all that motivated me, but I had other reasons for wanting to see Dalmannoch saved and developed as a cultural and spiritual centre – family tradition and sheer attachment to the place and to the people of Galloway, and if I may say so to yourselves. And you have to admit, everyone has benefited – the Gaelic group, the Wicca Coven, the MacPhedran Institute, increasingly the local community, and yes the Knights and of course yourselves."

Richard, admitted, a little reluctantly, that this was so.

Hector added:

"In normal circumstances, the Order would have carried on in secret without any of you being the wiser or the worse off. It is only because of recent events that I have had to break my vows and bring the three of you into our confidence, because we have work to do."

Hector looked once more at each in turn and then announced:

"I notice that in your own description of recent events, you have not mentioned Thomas Nutter. He has been in hiding for a week and I know you know of this. You see you have your own secret. I applaud you for keeping it."

There were more gasps from Hector's audience. It was Ruairidh who responded.

"How on earth did you know this Hector? We have been completely close-lipped about Thomas."

"Ah ha, we Elven Knights have our own channels of communication. Suffice it to say, I have had a message from Thomas, indirectly, that he is in danger and I plan to help him and at the same time bring Colin McCulloch's murderer or murderers to justice.

THE TRUSTEES' MEETING

ALL THOUGHTS OF ELVEN KNIGHTS and secret pledges were set aside the following morning, for Friday was the day scheduled for the meeting of the trustees of the Dalmannoch Foundation.

In Dalmannoch's library, the individual tables had been pushed together to form one large board-room table. Tea and coffee pots and cups were set out on a small side table. By half past ten, the seven trustees of the Dalmannoch Foundation were seated round the big table with three non-members also in attendance.

The agenda and papers had been circulated by email a week earlier. Some had paper copies before them. iPads or tablets were the mode of choice for others. Professor Ruairidh Alasdair Macdonald was in the chair.

"Welcome one and all to this the fifth full trustees' meeting of the Dalmannoch Foundation. We have quite a lot to get through, so let's make a start with the *Sederunt* - all present and correct – good."

The make-up of the meeting was as follows:

Trustees:
> Professor Ruairidh Alasdair Macdonald (Chairman)
> Hector Woodrow-Douglas
> Frances McGarrigle
> Gordon Douglas
> Holly Garden
> Catriona Macarthur
> Councillor Andrew Dunbar

In attendance:
> Brother Richard Wells (General Manager)
> Douglas Gordon (Secretary and Treasurer)
> James Arbuckle (Architect)

Catriona Macarthur was a solicitor with the Wigtown legal practice Agnew, Douglas and McWhirter. Andrew Dunbar was a local councillor, former close friend of the deceased lawyer Alexander Agnew and supporter of Dalmannoch.

The Professor proceeded through the agenda. There were no apologies for absence, the minutes of the previous meeting were approved and a number of matters arising from the minutes were discussed, including confirmation that Dalmannoch had been confirmed by the local authority under the Marriage (Scotland) Act 2002 to allow civil marriages to be conducted.

"Well this is good news", said Frances. "Weddings could be a major income stream for us, if we market ourselves properly. We have already had a number of couples making enquiries."

There was unanimous agreement that this was very positive progress.

The other important issue under 'Matters Arising' was the 'Brae Meadow', a large field belonging to the foundation that had been let out to a local farmer, Andrew Caruthers. The ten year lease was about to expire at Lammas. The future policy for this field generated a heated discussion in view of plans to be discussed later in the agenda for an ambitious phased building programme that would require a substantial area of land. It was Jamie Arbuckle who came to the rescue.

"If I may make a suggestion; whatever is agreed later today with regard to building work, it will take some time to get through the whole planning and building warrant process. I suggest the foundation lease the field to Andy Caruthers on a year by year basis. In that way, the foundation will continue to pull in some revenue until the timescale and land-take for building become clear. You can then either terminate the lease or re-lease either the whole or a smaller area of land to the farmer as may be appropriate at that time."

This sensible proposal was agreed.

A few further minor issues were covered after which arose the most important item on the agenda: 'The Future Direction of the Foundation'. The proposed plan was made up of three interlocked parts: business development, accommodation and finance.

Richard was first to be asked to make a presentation. His topic was development of the business. It may seem odd that an ex-monk be asked to handle such a subject matter, but Richard was practical, down-to-earth, had a wide range of experience and an incisive mind. His late father had run a building business and Richard had been a joiner, sailor, fisherman, and much else before becoming a monk. Even as a monk at Whitleigh Priory in the Cotswolds, where he had been responsible for building a bell tower, he had been inspired by the business acumen of his prior, Father John Ainslie.

Richard's presentation was to the point.

"The paper before you is a distillation of a good deal of informal discussion with most of you round this table and with others. In essence, Dalmannoch is not sustainable in its present form. We need more income generating activity – more critical mass. The potential new spheres of activity identified are: weddings, musical events and festivals, week-long residential courses in a range of skills such as creative writing, arts and crafts, outdoor pursuits and the like, and possibly workshop spaces for business that might be complimentary to these activities. All this would of course be in addition to our existing programme of conferences, seminars, Gaelic classes and spiritual endeavours. In achieving all this we need to put Dalmannoch on the map as a must-see destination – in other words good marketing. And of course we won't get there at all without more accommodation and finance."

A number of questions and a well-informed discussion followed, concluding in agreement that the proposition was a sound one subject to further research and to the practicality of creating more accommodation and financing it.

Jamie Arbuckle was next to have the floor. He spoke to a PowerPoint presentation in which options for creating more space at Dalmannoch were sketched out with ideas as to how such a development might be phased. He exemplified a 'design code' that would ensure that future building work was in sympathy with the existing buildings.

In the ensuing discussion it was agreed that, subject to finance, the two immediate priorities were a large flexible space that could be used as a dining hall or for receptions, dances or exhibitions and an accommodation block fitted with a mixture of comfortable en-suite rooms plus a bunk house for a total of up to say twenty persons. Jamie was then asked to work up some outline drawings with an indication of timescales and price parameters.

Then came the vital matter of finance. Duggie Gordon was at his most accountantish.

"The first point I'd like to make is that I agree with Brother Richard's assertion that Dalmannoch is unsustainable as it stands. Although we keep our costs to a minimum, and Brother Richard and Sister Frances are on the minimum wage, which in my opinion is unfair bearing in mind the quality of their work, our income from rentals, conference fees and such like does not cover our costs. Were it not for the generosity of Hector and a number of donations (some of them anonymous) and the input of our volunteers, we would be sunk.

At this point Richard butted in:

"When I was a monk, I had no income at all, so my current earnings are quite an improvement. Mind you, I can't say the same for Frances."

Duggie continued:

"I'm not going to argue the point, but as Brother Richard stressed in his presentation, we need a much enhanced income stream. The problem is that many of the ideas put forward require big capital expenditure on building work, money we do not have, and furthermore building work takes time.

The only way through this that I can see, is that we immediately identify a couple of money makers, using our current facilities, which will boost our cash flow and our credibility as a business. Then we may be in a position to raise capital. The two areas I suggest are weddings and a folk music festival. Smaller scale weddings we can handle in the chapel and dining room. We don't need much, if any, on-site accommodation for the festival other than camping space. We need to get the word out that we are a unique and romantic wedding venue with the multi-denominational/non-denominational chapel as the key selling point. A music festival will require a lot of organising, but I think the GGG and the Wicca Coven could rally round and we have a fair range of musical skills. We need a big name though. I'm a bit stuck there.

If we can pull this off, and if we are lucky, we may have the collateral to approach grant giving bodies such as the Lottery to assemble a funding package for our building programme. It's a big challenge.

All I would add is that a year ago, when we speculated on finding a way of taking over this building, I thought it was pie-in-the-sky; yet we did it. Maybe we can do it again."

There was a silence for a while, and then babble which the Chairman was eventually able to control and give each their say in turn. The upshot of the debate was that the trustees agreed the approach outlined by Duggie.

After closing the session and agreeing the date for the next meeting the company trooped through to the dining room for lunch.

* * *

While the meeting had been in progress, Suzie Silver had been busy in the kitchen preparing a buffet of salads, new potatoes, salmon, and cold meats. Suzie looked as glamorous as ever, in a short black dress, silver chain belt and silver high heeled sandals. Her smile was welcome relief from the formal atmosphere of the trustees meeting and a signal for the company to relax. One of the main topics of conversation, however, was the music festival, how it might be themed and what big name could be found to front it.

It was Suzie who came up with the most promising suggestion.

"How about Donnelly Dolan? He's back from LA and I heard he has bought a place in the borders, somewhere near Melrose. He is an active Pagan, although he keeps that quiet. I think we could maybe get him to do a gig here if we approach him through the Wicca network."

As had happened before at Dalmannoch, there was universal admiration for this unusual young woman's depths.

THE VALKYRIE

ONE WAY OR ANOTHER it had been an eventful week. True, Colin McCulloch's killer had not yet been uncovered, other than the claim by the missing Thomas Nutter that he apparently knew his or her identity. Neither had Colin's valuable notes come to light. The puzzle of the Eleven Knights had been resolved, however, and a new future was opening up for Dalmannoch. The postman's delivery of a card announcing that Colin's funeral would take place the following Thursday was at least a portent of some kind of closure.

The weekend beaconed and after lunch, the trustees of the Dalmannoch Foundation and their supporters went their separate ways. Professor Macdonald headed back north to the fastness of his Highland home, promising to return later the following week. Even Hector announced that he would be out for the rest of the afternoon and evening and would be back late.

For the first time in almost a week, Richard and Frances had Dalmannoch to themselves. Frances gave a sigh, partly of relief and partly of pleasure. She looked at Richard; smiled a mischievous smile and winked.

"Alone at last. Why don't we go for a wee lie down?"

Richard knew what a 'wee lie down' meant. He immediately felt a tingle of anticipation in his nether regions as the pair of them romped upstairs hand in hand to their bedroom and closed the door behind them.

* * *

It had been a relaxing weekend – a delightful humdrum of intimacy, shopping in Wigtown, walking on the beach, and on Richard's part, Sunday worship at St Aidan's.

The one extraordinary event from the outside world that deviated from the calm was the announcement on Saturday's news that Sir Crispin Short's financial empire had fallen apart. The financial supplement of the *Sunday Caledonian* was full of it, as Frances read under the heading 'No Future for Short Futures'. An in depth report by staff reporter Tony James described how a rogue trader had gambled close on a billion pounds to cover losses and come unstuck. The firm had been going through a bad patch and this disaster pushed it over the edge.

"I wonder what that means for Derrydruie and the wind farm project," speculated Brother Richard."

* * *

On Monday morning Hector, who had been doing his own thing for much of the weekend, joined Richard and Frances in the kitchen for breakfast. As they settled down to the meal, and after pleasantries, Hector came out with an unexpected announcement.

"I have been in contact with the Knights over the weekend and we have had an indirect communication from Thomas. He's planning to arrive at Isle of Whithorn later today by yacht."

"By yacht?" said Frances. "Where has he been?"

"I reckon we'll find out when we see him. My information is that he needs a safe hideaway, until Colin's murderer is outed. Of course, Dalmannoch would be the ideal place, but that would depend on you both being happy to shelter a fugitive."

Frances looked at Richard. Richard looked at Frances and then responded:

"I'd be up for it. I have never believed that Thomas was a murderer. No doubt we'll get a better idea who *is* when we see him. How about you Francie?"

"Fine by me."

Hector nodded in approval.

"OK, fine; we can keep him out of sight in my apartment if needs be and he can sleep in my guest bedroom. Now, in this whole operation discretion will be of the essence. Here's the plan . . ."

It was late morning when the three of them set off in Hector's Land Rover Discovery for the Isle with a packed lunch prepared by Frances. The Isle of Whithorn is not an island as such, but joined to the rest of the Machars peninsula by a causeway. Hector parked the vehicle at the car park just beyond the pier whereupon they all alighted. Before inspecting the harbour, Hector opened the glove compartment, extracted an A6 sized card bearing a solid green seven pointed star. With a felt tipped marker pen, he wrote on it the word 'Screwball' and placed it such that it was visible through the windscreen. The trio then checked out the boats in the harbour. It was half tide and several of the boats were still high and dry.

Satisfied that the vessel bearing Thomas had not yet arrived, Hector spoke.

"The boat we're looking for is called *Valkyrie*, so he hasn't arrived yet. I guess he'll be timing it for high tide. That's about half past two this afternoon. Let's wander up the hill to the Cairn and see if we can spot him."

And so the small group made their way to the prominent square white tower from which opened up a magnificent panorama of the Kirkcudbrightshire coast, the Cumbrian Fells and on the horizon to seaward, the hills of the Isle of Man.

Richard had a special regard for this place. It was here, just a year before, on his first morning in Scotland that he met Professor Ruairidh Alasdair Macdonald – the meeting that had led to his Dalmannoch adventure. Shading her eyes against the sun and the south-westerly breeze, to take in the distant island, Frances too was thinking about that adventure.

"Remember Richard, our trip to the Isle of Man and the lovely people we met – Juan Corlett, Fenella Qualtrough . . . I'd love to go back to spend a longer time there. Why don't we?"

"I'd like that too Francie, but let's get this business sorted first."

While Richard and Frances reminisced, Hector had pulled out his old but powerful Karl Zeiss binoculars to scan the expanse of the Irish Sea for a sighting of the *Valkyrie*. There was little maritime traffic to be seen. Quite close inshore, a fisherman in a small boat was checking and re-setting his lobster creels and in the far distance a container-ship hull-down headed east towards the Mersey. There were no yachts visible.

"I reckon we'll have to wait a-while before *Valkyrie* hoves in sight. Let's get on the outside of some chuck."

And with that the packed lunch was opened and the selection of prawn-mayo, ham and cheese sandwiches were consumed and washed down with coffee. Hector periodically scanned the horizon. It was not until the lunch things had been packed away that Richard cried:

"Look! There's a yacht coming in from the west round Burrow Head."

And it was so. A small white sloop rigged sailing yacht, some distance off, had appeared from beyond the headland on an easterly course. She was on a broad reach making good speed on the starboard tack. She continued on this course for some distance as though to by-pass the Isle of Whithorn altogether. Through his binoculars Hector could make out one man at the helm, then another appeared from below to take over the tiller, while the first made his way to the foredeck to make some adjustments. He returned to the cockpit and took over the helm once more.

Richard, as an ex sailor, was watching the proceedings with interest.

"He's preparing to gybe."

As he spoke, the yacht was turned to port and, as she passed through the eye-of-the-wind, the mainsail boom snapped over. The little vessel, now on the port tack, headed north straight for the inlet that forms the entrance to Isle of Whithorn's sheltered harbour. The ex sailor, ex monk approved.

"Thaat was nicely done." His West Country accent seemed just a little more pronounced as he lapsed into nautical mode. "Once she gets a bit closer we'll make out her name."

Hector kept his binoculars focussed on the bow of the vessel and, a minute or so later, he was able to make out the name *Valkyrie*.

"OK let's head back to the pier pronto before she berths."

By this time it was almost high water and as the trio walked smartly back to the harbour, the little yacht was making her way up the inlet with one man now on deck lowering and stowing the mainsail. The other was at the helm. The helmsman had the collar of his jacket fastened up tight and he wore sunglasses and a broad brimmed hat. The little craft had slowed under the drawing power of the foresail alone. By the time Richard, Frances and Hector had reached the pier, *Valkyrie* was making a broad sweep round the fairway to come up into the wind as the foresail was lowered and she slid alongside the pier. The bow line was thrown and caught and made fast by a bystander. The stern line was caught by Richard who also made it fast. Securely berthed, the man on deck checked that fenders were properly positioned and then scrambled ashore, the helmsman went below.

Hector by this time had returned to the Land Rover and sat in the driver's seat awaiting the next move. The sailor, a stocky pleasant looking fellow wearing a navy gansey, a yachtsman's smock, yellow rubber boots and a navy skipper's peaked cap, wandered along the harbour, firstly in the direction of the village, casually looking at the parked cars. Then he made his way back again to the car park. On spotting Hector's green star, he leaned in the driver's window and asked:

"Mr Douglas ?"

"Yes, I believe you have that screwball Mr Rettun on board."

"Yes I do, shall I ask him to come ashore?"

"Yes please do, I have some friends who are keen to help him."

And thus contact was made. Hector and the sailor returned to where the yacht was berthed. Richard and Frances were standing there on the quayside. The sailor went back aboard and disappeared below. After not more than a couple of minutes, he and 'Mr Rettun' stepped ashore to meet up with Hector, Richard and Frances. 'Mr Rettun', hat pulled well down over his face, sporting ten days dark stubble and 'Aviator' dark glasses, was of course none other than a somewhat disguised Thomas Nutter.

THOMAS'S TALE

THOMAS WAS ESCORTED by his friends to Hector's vehicle, in which, the group made their way directly to Dalmannoch. The skipper of the *Valkyrie*, Terry O'Donnell, had been invited along but declined the offer. He did not want to loose the tide.

On the way to Dalmannoch, Frances suggested ringing Holly Garden and Suzie and Gordon Douglas to invite them round to meet Thomas. This was agreed so long as the invitation was couched in oblique terms in case of a tap on the mobile phone.

On arrival at Dalmannoch, Hector showed Thomas to his quarters in the apartment's spare bedroom where he was invited to freshen up. After a shower and a change of clothes, the fugitive joined the group in the kitchen. Tea and coffee were poured and a plate of cakes circulated, by which time Holly arrived.

"Thomas! I'm so glad to see you. How are you? We were all so concerned."

Thomas was his usual stoical self. "Oh I'm all right. Glad to be back after all that has transpired."

"Where have you been?"

"Well I'll tell you all the whole story once Suzie and Gordon arrive.

As he spoke these words, the said pair arrived amid more expressions of welcome, hugs and concern. With the arrival of Suzie and Gordon, all those who were in on the circumstances of Thomas's disappearance were now present, apart from Professor Macdonald and Douglas Gordon, who was away on business, and an unknown number of the Elven Knights' network.

It was Richard who brought some focus to the situation.

"Well Thomas, now that we're all here, let's have your story."

Thomas slurped a mouthful of tea, brushed some cake crumbs from his shirt and began his account of events from his perspective.

"Well I need to go back in time. As some of you probably know, Colin and I didn't see eye to eye on – how can I put it – the validity of modern Paganism as practiced by us in the Wicca Coven. I like to think I'm normally a composed kind of fellow, but Colin didn't realise how much his mocking hurt.

You see; when I was a young man, I was in the Royal Marines and I was stationed for a time in Northern Ireland on special duties. Against my wife Lily's better judgement, I had arranged for her to join me in Belfast. Our son David was just a tiny baby and I just wanted my family near me."

Thomas paused, clearly struggling with his emotions.

"I haven't told any of you this before, except for Holly, but while I was on deployment, Lily and my baby son were caught in cross-fire between Loyalists and Republicans."

Thomas paused again; swallowed hard and continued.

"They were both shot. David was killed instantly; Lily was taken to hospital but died before I could get to her bed-side.

Thomas, stopped, looked upwards, fought for composure, his voice broke.

"I was devastated. They meant everything to me. I wanted to settle the score, but how could I? Lily and my baby son were the victims of two groups professing Christianity but preaching hate – a curse on both their houses!

I went through a bad patch until I was introduced to Wicca by a man who became a very good friend over the years – Paddy Stewart. He has a small farm in the Sperrins. Paddy helped me turn my life round with the Ancient Religion as my guiding principle. As it happens I have since discovered that I am related to Alice Nutter one of the, so called, Pendle Witches – innocent women healers who were tried and executed in Lancaster for witchcraft in 1612.

That's the reason I take my beliefs so seriously and why Colin's insults bit so deeply.

Then a few weeks ago our rapport changed for the better. This was due in part to your intervention Brother Richard. You advised me to 'rubber ear' Colin's remarks and I know you told Colin to back off. The thaw was also due to events at Derrydruie.

As you will all know, there was an editorial in the *Gazette* a few weeks ago describing plans by a businessman – what's his name – George Lang – for a ghastly theme park at Derrydruie. I was appalled at the idea. Derrydruie is an ancient spiritual site with a healing well of special significance to Pagans throughout the south of Scotland and beyond. I put the word out round the Pagan network and I was by no means alone in my concerns. Then I chanced to meet Colin who was also on the warpath about, what he described as, the desecration of Derrydruie. From that point we joined forces. Colin actually apologised about his behaviour towards me. I was astonished at that. He wasn't normally one to show contrition. The long and the short of it was he set up an action group to stop the development and preserve the wood. Then between us a gathering at Derrydruie was planned and publicised via Facebook and Twitter and word of mouth among the various groups who were likely to have an interest in the campaign."

As Thomas paused for breath, Richard added that they were aware of Colin's involvement in the Derrydruie campaign and had come to realise that there had been a rapprochement.

"What we are anxious to hear is what you know about Colin's murder."

Thomas continued. "I'm coming to that if you will bear with me.

The gathering took place and it attracted a surprising variety of participants, Pagans of course, Greens, wildlife enthusiasts, twitchers, heritage devotees, New Age folk and many quite ordinary citizens. Speeches were made and there was much mutual agreement on the need to protect Derrydruie when three police cars and a van, sirens wailing, screeched to a halt at the gate to the woodland and a squad of uniformed cops with batons rushed into the gathering. Through a loud hailer the senior man ordered the meeting to disperse. Silence was followed by murmurings, which were followed by questions by key participants on the grounds for the police action, then by angry arguments, not least by Colin. Soon a few scuffles broke out and the police started to lay into the gathering.

I took the view that discretion was the better part of valour. I tried to persuade Colin to leave, but he was intent on protesting to the police. I sloped off uphill and lay in the undergrowth watching events from a position above the well. Professor Osmond who had come along to show support, and seeing that matters were getting out of hand, tried to calm the situation but was hit by a police baton and arrested. Other arrests were made of so called ringleaders, including Colin and eventually the assembly dispersed. I was able to slip away unobserved.

We later discovered that the landowner Sir Crispin Short had heard of the gathering and asked the police to stop what he claimed was 'the malicious damage to his property being perpetrated by rioters'.

This was of course untrue. It was a well behaved gathering who wished to preserve the woodland, certainly not to damage it. In the end, those arrested were not charged and the inspector, a man called Huxtable, who led the raid, was made to look rather foolish."

At this point Frances chipped in:

"Huxtable! From what Richard and Ruairidh tell me, the man's an idiot and bad news generally."

"Mmm, well this brings me to the night Colin was killed.

Colin and I set off late that warm afternoon, on his motor bike, with me on the pillion, for a meeting in Dumfries with the Derrydruie Action Group. After our meeting we visited Colin's girlfriend Minnie. She lives in Dumfries too. Although it was getting late, it was a mild evening, there was a full moon and Colin had a notion to visit Sweetheart Abbey. One of the Action Group, a woman called Felicity Riddell, had said the rose window at the choir end of the abbey had originally been in the shape of a seven pointed star so we thought we would check that out while we were in the area.

Colin had had a couple of drinks at Minnie's. I had just tea, so I drove the bike and Colin sat pillion. We motored over to New Abbey and, so as not to draw attention to ourselves, we parked the bike in a side lane near the bridge over the New Abbey Pow. We walked through the village. It must have been about eleven by then and there was no one around. We skirted round the edge of the abbey perimeter and climbed over the wall into the grounds. In the bright moonlight, it was easy to find our way across to the nave and into the building. We walked towards the choir and the altar to get a good view of the semi-circular window above the main window on the eastern gable.

At first sight it appeared as a big opening. The stone tracery that may have formed the seven pointed star was missing, except for a few hanging fragments. We talked in whispers, but from these we thought it might be imagined that they represented the points of a star but concluded that whatever the design it was not a seven pointed star. It seemed like a fool's errand.

Then we heard muffled voices. They seemed to be emanating from one of the ruined out buildings. We walked over to investigate. We were shocked at what we saw.

A young girl, she couldn't have been more that twelve or thirteen, was being held down by two men. One, with his trousers down was on top of her in the sex act. The other knelt to hold down her shoulders. The girl's mouth was covered with a plaster.

I don't know who was more surprised, them or us. For a moment no one moved.

The kneeling man looked up at me and then at Colin. Then he said 'McCulloch – what the devil! . . .'

Colin also recognised the man.

'Huxtable!'

The other man had by this time stood up and struggled to pull up his trousers. I leant down to ask the girl if she was all right.

She tried to struggle free but was still pinned down by Huxtable. She looked at me with terrified eyes.

And then bang – stars – I was out for the count!"

FUGITIVE

THERE WERE GASPS OF INCREDULITY round the kitchen table at Dalmannoch. Richard was the first to give voice.

"Huxtable?! Inspector Huxtable?! Good heavens! I didn't like the man, but I never suspected he was that depraved."

There was a general hubbub and it was Suzie who asked.

"What happened next Thomas. You were knocked out?"

"I don't know how long I was unconscious, but when I came to, my head hurt like blazes, my hands and legs were bound and my mouth was gagged. I looked around and I was on my own in the same ruined out building we had stumbled on Huxtable, his associate and the girl.

I tried to move and found I could sit up and edge my back against a wall. My hands were bound tight behind my back and I couldn't reach my feet. They weren't bound quite so tightly. I managed to hook the cord round the sharp edge of stone and after rubbing and pulling the knot slipped and I was able to stand. I listened and heard voices. I crept quietly, following the sound in the direction of the choir. Just as I peered round the side entrance, I was horrified with what I saw. The two men had bound and gagged Colin, held him down lying on the slab that marked the position of the altar. Huxtable plunged a long dagger into Colin's heart."

Several of those round the table winced and Holly in particular was visibly shaken.

"Oowh! How dreadful. Poor Colin."

Thomas raised his arms as a sign of frustration.

"I could do nothing to save him.

Huxtable seemed in control, but the other man was clearly distressed.

'My God ! Who would have thought it would come to this ? Mark my words', he said, 'we'll regret this night.'

I couldn't make out the next bit properly, but Huxtable was getting impatient.

'Shut up Winkle', or Winkie or something like that, he said, 'We've dealt with the girl and McCulloch. Now we need to sort out the other fellow, then we're in the clear.'

Well with that, I decided to make myself scarce.

Bear in mind, I still had my hands tied behind my back, but, as a marine, I know how to move fast and silently. I ran down the row of out buildings then doubled back round the rear of the choir and got over the perimeter wall before they realised I was gone. From my vantage point behind the shadow of the wall I could watch them searching for me. They were clearly in a panic. Eventually they gave up and I heard a car start and drive off in the direction of the coast."

The group round the table looked at each other agog. Frances was the next to butt in.

"What happened to the girl? I suppose she must have been put in the car. I wonder if that's the same young girl, from the Craigdoune Childrens' Home, whose body was washed up at Southerness. Poor lassie."

Thomas had not read the press report, but presumed that it may well have been the same girl.

"There was certainly no sign of her when I made my bid for freedom. However, after the car was out of earshot, I made my way back through the village to the bridge over the New Abbey Pow. I managed to get down to the water's edge looking for something sharp to cut the cord binding my hands – something that might have been chucked over the bridge. The best I could find was a sharp stone. I worked at it rubbing. Eventually the cord gave way.

I ripped off the plaster from my mouth and headed for Colin's motor bike. Fortunately I still had the ignition key in my pocket. I pushed the bike out of the village until I was more or less out of earshot, started her and headed over the by-road for Beeswing and then on to the main road west.

By the time I reached Elven Cottage (Thomas's house just outside Wigtown), it was five in the morning and daylight. I washed, changed, quickly packed a few things, put some food and water down for Tiddles (Thomas's cat) and set off again. I took some cash out from the auto-teller in Wigtown and high-tailed it for Cairnryan. There's a man I know there, an ex marine, Sammy Caruthers, that I called on. It was six o' clock and I got him out of his bed, explained that I was on the run and could he hold on to Colin's motor bike and keep quiet about it. This he agreed.

I mosied down to the P&O ferry terminal and booked passage on the half past seven boat for Larne with cash. Once I was at sea, I felt safer, although I was pretty hopeful that Huxtable and the other man didn't know who I was. I had a leisurely breakfast on board and when I arrived at Larne, I went to a public phone box to ring my old pal Paddy Stewart to see if he could put me up for a few days on his farm. He was happy, in fact delighted to do so. We hadn't met up for years. I hung around Larne for a bit and then caught the half past eleven bus to Ballymena. Paddy picked me up at about half past twelve at George's Square and we got to his place at the back of one in time for lunch.

You should see his place. It's in the Glenelly Valley; absolutely idyllic. Actually his house is small and a bit run down and so is his farm. It's a smallholding really, but the setting is beautiful, peaceful and secret with small fields separated by hedgerows. The house catches the sun and nestles under Sawel Mountain. It just makes you feel good to be there.

Anyway, it was great to catch up with Paddy. I was able to fill him in on events of the previous twenty four hours and to rely on his discretion. He is an interesting character. On top of our mutual Pagan interests, he is very knowledgeable about the heritage of the Sperrins and has learned Irish Gaelic which was quite generally spoken in the area until relatively recent times. To practice he goes over to a place called Carntogher which is a kind of centre for the Irish language, a bit like Dalmannoch is for Scottish Gaelic.

Well, after a few days at Paddy's place, helping him with his chores, I recovered my equilibrium. Then I realised that people here might be wondering where I was."

"You bet we were," Frances affirmed. "We were really worried and considering reporting you missing, but we hung fire. Wouldn't it have been awful if we had tipped off Inspector Huxtable and made you his prime suspect or fall guy?"

"I'm sorry, I should have made contact sooner, but I didn't know how the land lay and wondered if the phones were tapped. That's why I phoned Gordon's office and as it happened got through to Suzie. Just as well, eh?

The rest of the story you can guess. On my return to Scotland, I wanted to keep a low profile, so Paddy made contact with his friend Terry O'Donnell to see if he would take me across in the *Valkyrie*, which was agreed and I contacted Sammy Caruthers to see if he could arrange for me to be met at this end."

For the first time as this long saga unfolded, Hector spoke.

"You may not know that Sammy is an old friend of mine too – em – part of my – em – network, so to speak. That's how we established communication and a welcome party at the Isle."

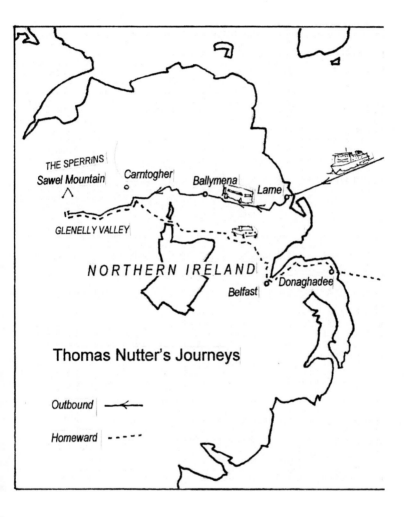

THE SPERRINS

Sawel Mountain Carntogher Ballymena Larne

GLENELLY VALLEY

NORTHERN IRELAND

Belfast Donaghadee

Thomas Nutter's Journeys

Outbound ⟵

Homeward - - - -

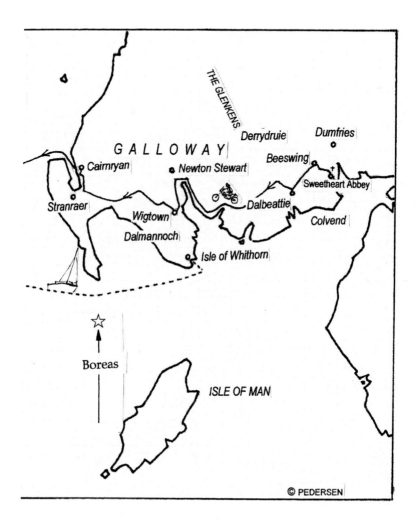

Everyone looked at Hector in awe of his amazing influence.

Thomas continued.

"So really, that brings me up to date. Paddy drove me to Donaghadee in the wee small hours and we set out in *Valkyrie* from Donaghadee early this morning. The rest you know. Here I am."

"Michty me," exclaimed Gordon in his Broad Scots and not noted for unnecessary verbosity; "That's some yarn. I widna hae believed it, gin I had read it in a buik. Ye mon be fair wabbit wi aa that traivellin."

Thomas had to admit that he was somewhat tired and would welcome an early night.

There was much further discussion and questioning by the group of Thomas, and by Thomas of the group, as to what had been happening among the Dalmannoch folk over the previous week and a half. Before anyone knew it, it was time for Dinner. Frances and Suzie set to preparing a meal in fit celebration of Thomas's safe return.

Over the meal discussion turned to what needed to be done about bringing Colin's murderer, or murderers to book.

Then the front door bell rang. It was the Reverend Donald Angus MacLeod and another man. He looked unusually grave.

"Can I introduce, Willie Christie, one of my elders? As Richard knows, Willie managed to get an inside track on the Elect of the Revelation. He has just been contacted by one of the Elect members. It's bad news. Willie you'd better describe what is to happen."

"Good evening all, I'm sorry not to be the bearer of better tidings, but I was phoned tonight by one of the Elect to ask me to join them on a planned raid on Dalmannoch. They intend to burn the place down – tonight!

PREPARING FOR BATTLE

AFTER WHAT HAD BEEN an unusually eventful day of surprises, this latest bombshell, delivered from the lips of Willie Christie, caused consternation round the Dalmannoch kitchen table.

Frances was infuriated. "Are these people completely off their heads? What are they trying to achieve?"

The Reverend Donald Angus confirmed that they were indeed 'off their heads'. He went on:

"These kinds of religious fanatics are oblivious to the major evils of the world: poverty, criminality, exploitation and such like. They focus instead, to the point of hatred, on those of spiritual persuasions that are not exactly like their own. They especially revile groups who embrace free, tolerant and enquiring spirits such as our diverse community at Dalmannoch."

Having digested the news, the ever practical Brother Richard spoke.

"Well, if this raid is to take place tonight, we better prepare ourselves. We need to phone the local police and in the meantime prepare to defend ourselves."

"Well done Richard," said Hector, "to the point as usual. We need a plan of action. Many a military tactician will tell you that the best form of defence is attack." He turned to Willie.

"Willie, what do you know of this raid? Do you know how many men they have, how will they get here and when? And do they have a plan of attack?

"Well I haven't got detailed information, but I was told that a bus would be coming down from Troon, picking people up on the way and they plan to arrive at about three in the morning when they presume everyone will be fast asleep. As I understand it they intend to rush the building and throw Molotov cocktails through the windows to set the place afire."

At this point Holly, who, in her innocence, was not well versed in weaponry, asked:

"I've heard of Molotov cocktails, but what exactly are they".

It was Hector who explained.

"A Molotov cocktail, Holly, is a simple incendiary device hurled at the target. It's a glass bottle filled with gasoline, I mean petrol, and a lighted wick. When the bottle smashes on impact, the petrol ignites, causing a fireball – simple but very effective."

That point being clarified, Willie continued with his intelligence report.

"I don't know how many there will be, but a bus suggests not more than about forty. I do know that there will be a couple of nasty ex URHS men, that's the Ulster Red Hand Squad. One of them is Bulldog Billy Smith who seems to front a number of security companies operating in the west of Scotland. He lives in Troon. Then there's Sammy (the Sadist) Black. He runs a used car dealership in Paisley (the two of them had been in the Maze together). That's about as much as I can tell you.

By the way I made my excuses to say that I couldn't participate. Of course, Donald and I'll stay with you here to mount our defence. If you want us, that is."

"You bet. We need every man we can rally."

"And woman" chipped in Suzie, Holly and Frances in unison.

"Sure thing ladies! And woman."

Hector continued:

"That's very useful information, Willie. I presume they won't know that we know their plans and hope to have surprise on their side. It seems to me we need to do two things – get reinforcements and plan a counter attack to head them off before they get within range of the house and chapel. Let's make some phone calls."

Hector and Richard went through to the reception room to phone. Richard lifted the instrument.

"It's dead!"

He turned to the computer and wiggled the mouse.

"The internet's off too. The wires must have been cut. And of course we have no mobile phone reception here."

They returned to the kitchen to report the latest development.

"Right," Hector announced, "I'm going out to rustle up help".

Donald then chimed in.

"I'll go out too to see how many of the Gaelic Group I can rally."

Then it was Richard who spoke. "That's great, and please be quick, but before you go, I have been thinking. If we want to head them off wouldn't we be best to attack them in the wood before they come within range of our buildings. I think I know how we could do that. What do you think?"

"First class Richard. While we're out, go right ahead and plan our counter attack, but make sure you let us back in before you put the attack into action."

Richard stood to attention and made a mock salute, with a "Yes sir" to Hector who had undoubtedly assumed the function of General.

"OK, OK. Stand easy. Let's get this show on the road." And with that Hector and the Reverend Donald Angus departed.

Richard's stratagem was quite simple. As the drive into the Dalmannoch policies leaves the road, it passes through a wood for a couple of hundred yards. The plan was to create a barrier across the road at about a third of the way into the wood, forcing the assailants to alight and make their way forward on foot. The defenders meantime would hide in the wood and, at the appropriate signal, attack with missiles to disorientate the representative of the Elect of the Revelation to their discomfort and hopefully put them to flight. The missiles would be manufactured during the course of the evening. To form the barrier, Richard had selected a substantial birch tree by the side of the drive that was already dying and covered in ivy. He planned to fell this so that it would lie across the drive.

Outside the house and chapel, the vehicles of the defenders would be turned to face the drive and the wood, so that at another signal, their lights would be switched on to illuminate the attackers.

Preparations were made to this effect.

It was some time before the first of the reinforcements arrived, but by dribs and drabs, they did. Such was the mutual energy and excitement that evening, that there is now no exact agreement as to the order in which they did arrive, but by eleven o' clock Jonathan Hepburn, a member of the Wigtown Wicca Coven had joined the party and from the Gaelic Group, the Reverend Donald Angus, Duggie Gordon, Iain Stewart, the Craigs, Cuddie McGrotty, Angus and Fiona Martin and most usefully Peggy McKie, accompanying her farmer father Sandy McKie on a large green John Deere tractor equipped with front loading forks and pulling a muck spreader.

In the course of the evening everyone had been busy manufacturing munitions and defensive materiel. Branches were selected in the wood and fashioned into clubs, for strictly defensive use only. The women were occupied in the kitchen grinding pepper of which there was unfortunately a limited supply and making flour bombs. The garden strawberries were stripped of their netting. Ropes, string and wire were selected from the out-buildings and cached. Sandy McKie's muck spreader was an unexpected bonus.

"Wiel, Brither Richard," Sandy averred in his rich Scots, "gin thae fanatics cam ower close, I'll gie them a skoosh o slurry. They'll nae muckle like that. It'll lea' a bit o a stink mind, fur a week or twa, bit losh, it'll fair mak the gress green."

"I can only say Sandy that I'm delighted you could come, and although I'm normally a man of peace, I approve of Dalmannoch's new weapon of mass destruction."

At half-past eleven, Richard called a meeting. The atmosphere in the common room was one of excited anticipation. Richard counted the number of those present and then addressed them.

"Friends; thank you all for answering the call to fight for Dalmannoch's survival. It seems that the Elect of the Revelation have an intense dislike for Dalmannoch and what it and its supporters stand for. Our inside source (thank you Willie) informs us that tonight they intend to burn down our building or buildings. Fortunately we believe they are unaware that we know their plans. This gives us two advantages. One: they have lost the element of surprise, and two: by preparing our defence, *we* have the element of surprise on our side. We don't know how many of them there are – perhaps thirty or forty. We are now eighteen in number and I hope that Hector may shortly arrive with a few more. We don't know exactly when they will arrive. Willie thinks about three a.m., but we must be prepared and in our positions well before that. Now here are the posts I have allocated to each of you . . ."

At that Richard instructed each where they were to be stationed in the forthcoming affray and what their duties were to be.

By midnight Brother Richard and Gordon Douglas were preparing to fell the birch tree that had been selected as a road-block. A number of the spreading limbs were quickly severed by Richard's chain saw, while Gordon passed a rope round one of the main vertical branches.

As Richard was cutting a notch into the trunk to control the direction in which the tree would fall, he was startled by the sound of a vehicle turning into the drive. It was a grey Land Rover Discovery; the vehicle of Hector Woodrow-Douglas. It stopped beside the two woodsmen and a smiling Hector stuck his head out of the window.

"Hector ! You frightened the life out of me. I thought Pastor Mutch's gang had arrived early."

"I don't think they'll be here for a few hours yet, but best get the road block in place as soon as possible. I have another car load behind me. Is everyone else here?"

"Yes I think so."

"Right. We'll take our cars up to the house and once you have finished here we can talk tactics."

The Land Rover was followed by a silver grey Lexus saloon within which four figures were faintly discernable in the darkness.

In no time the tree was felled across the drive and Richard and Gordon returned to the common room which was the nerve centre of the defence operation.

They were met by a weird and wonderful sight. There, standing in splendour, were seven men, each wearing tan riding boots and a green mantle bearing a silver Elven Star, each, except for Hector wore a silver-grey knitted balaclava, reminiscent of chain mail, which concealed most of their faces. Under the left arm, each held a helmet and in the right hand each held a long mahogany baton, except for Hector who held a Remington hunting rifle. Hector introduced the newcomers.

"Richard, these are the Elven Knights at your service and ready for battle. I brought this fire-stick along just in case any of our unwelcome guests are foolish enough to bear firearms. I've got a powerful searchlight and a loud-hailer in the car too. They might come in handy."

Richard, in common with the rest of the defenders was somewhat stuck for words.

"All I can say is welcome. We have some food and drinks in the kitchen. Do please help yourselves and then we must take up our positions.

ATTACK AND COUNTER ATTACK

THE MINUTES AND THE HOURS seemed interminable. The mood was expectant, but sombre. Although it was summer, the night had become cold. There was dampness in the air. The waning crescent moon shed little light, especially for those stationed in the wood. Yawns were stifled. Cold arms and legs were rubbed to stimulate circulation.

It was about a quarter past three when the faint sound of a diesel engine was heard, as yet perhaps a mile away in the still of the night. The sound became louder as its source approached and within a couple of minutes, a deceleration and gear change. A vehicle had turned into the drive only to stop a few moments later as the fallen tree was reached.

The bus's side door opened and a couple of figures emerged to contemplate the blockage. They made a half-hearted attempt to shift it, but that was clearly hopeless. They re-entered the bus wherein a faint murmur of voices could just be heard over the rumble of the engine. Then the engine was switched off.

The side door opened again and figures emerged one by one. They assembled in a group of about thirty. Most held a bottle – a deadly bottle, affixed to the neck of which was a tell-tale fuse of meths soaked cloth.

The defenders held their breaths, watched and listened. Acrimonious voices conveyed that the attackers were by no means happy with the situation in which they found themselves.

"But you said we would get the bus right up to the house. Hit and run you said; then turn around and offski. Now we'll have to reverse the bus back down the drive in the dark."

"Aw shut yer face. Yer aye moanin'. There's nae problem. They'll aw be in their beds. A walk up the drive'll dae us nae hairm."

Then a more commanding if rather high pitched voice.

"Brethern, hear my words. This night's work is for the greater glory of the Lord our God. We are soldiers of God and the wiles of the Devil are our enemy. We fight against the rulers of darkness in this world and wickedness in high places. Stay ye not, but pursue after our enemies, and smite the hindmost of them; suffer them not to enter into their cities: for the Lord your God hath delivered them into our hand. And yea bretheren we lift up the sword of righteousness against Paganism, Popery, Prelacy, Malignancy and Sectarianism that are anathema to the Lord. Go forth. He will protect us from this evil."

Then, in a gruff Belfast accent; a more practical note.

"Have youse all got lighters?"

There was a general murmured affirmation that the assembled forces were so equipped, after which they clambered over the fallen tree and proceeded towards the Dalmannoch buildings.

As the defenders watched the progress of the invaders, Jonathan Hepburn, who, besides his Wiccan interests, was a keen amateur dramatist and mimic, let out a gentle "woooo" in realistic imitation of an owl.

The invaders stopped.

"What was that?"

"Ach, it's just a hoolet. You dinna hae thaim in Kilmarnock. Noo shut up."

Then, deeper in the wood, on the other side of the drive, Cuddie McGrotty sought to further un-nerve the raiders with a dog-like "grrrrr".

"That wiz a dug. This place gies me the Willies."

A few more yards in the direction of the house, then a hunting horn sounded. A dozen of the defenders, hidden on each side of the drive emitted yells and screams and the war-cry "Dail Manach gu Brath". They hurled paper bags of flour at the intruders.

A panic overtook the raiders. Some made to double back to the bus, but blocking their way, and advancing towards them, illuminated by a spotlight, was a helmeted and cloaked Elven Knight wielding his lethal baton. He was accompanied by six defenders with rough clubs.

"Not this way my friends. Move forward."

The Knight's command was readily heeded and the frightened and disorientated Zealots turned, dropping bottles as they went and started to run up the drive away from the uncanny cloaken apparition, and the bus.

Then a disembodied but urgent order was heard from within the wood.

"If any try to leave the drive, shoot to kill! I repeat: shoot to kill!"

And from the other side of the wood a loud bang (a firework actually) and: "Hold your fire man!"

Seconds later, the wail of the Reverend Donald Angus MacLeod's pipes rent the night air with a medley of regimental marches – Hielan Laddie, March of the Cameron Men and Scotland the Brave. The bewildered insurgents were herded along the drive, but before reaching the open lawn, a strawberry net was cast over a goodly number and as they stumbled and fell over each other, cords were drawn and some half dozen were caught in a bag with Jonathan Hepburn standing over them with a particularly nasty looking club in his hand.

"The first one to move a muscle will feel the end of this."

Quite a number of the raiders made it through the wood and as they emerged, several defenders darted forward aiming for their faces with pepper pellets.

"Ow, ahh, f—in Hell I canna see. Ow."

Still the more determined of the unwelcome visitors pressed on towards the house with bottles in hand at which point a car horn sounded and an array of full beam headlights illuminated the white flour covered figures. A tractor engine started and a spray of brown and very smelly liquid was directed from the muck spreader towards the advancing invaders, already much reduced in numbers.

"Ehh, gads, for f—s sake. What's this? Come on, let's get out of here."

There was one large man among the raiders who seemed to elude the Dalmannoch defences. By his bald tattooed head he was subsequently identified by the Reverend Donald Angus as none other than Bulldog Billy

Smith, who, it has to be said, showed more guts than the rest of the Elect of the Revalation's hapless forces. He ran, lit Molotov cocktail in hand, towards Dalmannoch's chapel, but he was picked out in the beam of a blinding searchlight mounted on a Land Rover Discovery. A loud hailer blared in a commanding Canadian voice.

"Stop! Don't take one step further or I'll shoot you."

Bulldog Billy carried on lit Molotov cocktail in hand. A rifle shot rang out and a bullet whistled over his head.

"You have been warned. Next time I'll aim for your black heart. Lay down your weapon now and move slowly backwards from it."

With that, Billy complied. The bottle was placed on the ground and Billy backed away slowly. The ground was uneven and the bottle with its still burning fuse toppled over. The cap can't have been securely fixed for after a few seconds there was a flash and a fire-ball of exploding petrol that knocked Billy from his feet.

A process ensued of rounding up Pastor Erskine Mutch's flock, aided by the waving of knobbly clubs and the subtler, but more intimidating, presence of the Elven Knights. There were a few further minor skirmishes and scuffles, here and there between insurgents and defenders, but before long the raiding party was corralled in the middle of the lawn surrounded by the club wielding friends of Dalmannoch.

At the centre of this disconsolate group was Pastor Erskine Mutch himself, a pathetic creature, covered in stinking brown sharn.

TRUCE

DAWN BROKE as the defenders of Dalmannoch assessed the outcome of their nocturnal efforts. Most importantly, Dalmannoch had been saved from destruction. There was a nursing of scratches and bruises on both sides, but amazingly, there were no serious casualties. Even Bulldog Billy Smith, while suffering minor burns and cuts, was still in one piece.

Brother Richard approached defeated raiders who were now seated or lying on the lawn. They presented a mixed and bedraggled appearance, some flour white, others brown, wet and very smelly. All were clearly cold and looking very sorry for themselves.

"Pastor Much, it's time to parley. Do I take it that you and your forces are willing formally to surrender and cease belligerent action against Dalmannoch's buildings, effects and personnel? Your bus has been immobilised and it is no doubt a long walk back from whence you came."

Pastor Erskine Mutch's eyes betrayed a deep fear and humiliation, most likely because of loss of face in front of his disciples rather than martial defeat as such. He looked for support from those around him, but the fight was out of them. He found none, but could not bring himself to speak.

Brother Richard looked hard at the pastor.

"We seek peace. We will not harm you or your men so long you give us your word as a Christian that your followers will cease hostilities forthwith and that you are prepared, in their interest to discuss terms. You will find us more merciful than I suspect you would have been, had the tables been turned.

I repeat. Do you and your forces agree to cease hostilities? Do you agree to talk?"

Murmurs among the cold and miserable captives were clearly directed at urging the pastor to agree. The pastor rose to his feet, and summoning as much limited dignity as his small excrement covered form could muster, he spoke.

"I so agree."

Brother Richard nodded and in a soft but firm voice he indicated with his hand the direction of the Dalmannoch buildings.

"If you would be good enough Pastor Mutch to come this way please. I'm sure we can come to an understanding among ourselves in a civilised manner."

The pastor meekly followed the ex-monk towards the chapel and on reaching the entrance, Richard asked politely.

"Would you please remove your shoes. We don't want leave a trail of – er, mud do we?"

Once inside, the pastor saw some figures sitting round a small table placed in front of the high altar and the unique, magical and rich decorative scheme within. He bridled.

"I will not enter a house of the Antichrist."

As he made to withdraw, Richard gently suggested:

"Perhaps you would rather we sent for the police, for them to consider the facts and for you and your followers to face charges of arson and attempted murder. My colleagues have been carefully collecting the bottles your people were carrying, each with fine sets of fingerprints. I'm sure the police would be most interested if we were to make them available. However, I don't think it need come to that."

The pastor hesitated and weighing up his options, he must have decided that waiving his principles on this one occasion was preferable to the possibility of a long prison sentence.

"In the circumstances, I am prepared to meet with you here." In an attempt to regain a little authority, he added. "We in the Elect of the Revelation, are well connected with the police at senior level. In fact Detective Inspector Alexander Huxtable is an active member of our congregation."

Brother Richard raised his eyebrows and as the pair walked up the aisle towards the seated group he commented politely.

"Interesting. However, I have my doubts that even the great powers of Inspector Huxtable would be able to alter the course of justice, should charges be brought. Now let me introduce you to the representatives of the trustees of the Dalmannoch Foundation."

Seated at the table were the Reverend Donald Angus MacLeod, Holly Garden, Hector Woodrow Douglas, who had by now shed his Knight's attire and reverted in form to a conventional business man, and Douglas Gordon who it was explained, as Secretary and Treasurer of the Dalmannoch Foundation, would take notes of the peace negotiations. Standing behind the table and in front of the high altar was an Elven Knight in full attire, standing easy with baton held loosely, but ready for action should the need arise.

Each, apart from the Elven Knight bowed slightly as their name was mentioned and Hector took up his accustomed role as chairman. A chair had been prepared for the pastor facing the trustees. It had been covered with black plastic bags to protect it from being soiled.

"Please be seated Pastor Mutch and thank you for agreeing to discuss peace terms with us. Perhaps I should start by explaining that we at Dalmannoch are a spiritual and cultural foundation based on principles of peace and tolerance. In the interests of maintaining a fair and balanced settlement with the Elect of the Revelation, I have

147

asked one of the Galloway Knights of Peace, who aided us this morning to observe our proceedings and to ensure fair play. Their motto is *pax et iustitia* (peace and justice). You can be assured of his discretion. Now perhaps you will be kind enough to explain why you and your followers felt it necessary to attack us. Mmm?"

The pastor, normally so sure of his ground, was completely wrong-footed by the exaggerated politeness of his inquisitors.

"Well we – em – we are – em – we are devout Christians who are led by the word of the Lord our God as set out in Holy Scripture. These Holy words are our guide. The national churches no longer preach the true Word and we are surrounded by the depravity of unbelievers and sinners. The Elect of the Revelation commands all men to repent and believe, for the wicked shall be turned into Hell."

Hector held up his hand.

"I didn't ask for a sermon on the evils of the world Pastor Mutch. I think we are all agreed here that there is much sin and depravity to be found, but why pick on Dalmannoch. We have done you no harm surely."

"Dalmannoch is a nest of Pagans, Catholics and unbelievers. One of your people – Colin McCulloch publicly denounced and ridiculed the Elect of the Revelation in the newpapers. We cannot stand to be humiliated in this way."

At this point Richard sought the chairman's permission to speak.

"Pastor Mutch, Colin McCulloch was a gifted fellow at the MacPhedran Institute. It is true he had an abrasive manner and ridiculed many within, as well as outside, Dalmannoch. In many ways this was annoying, but freedom of speech is a hard won right and we respect that. We did not seek drastic retribution for Colin's rejoinders.

However, Colin was murdered some ten days ago. It is strange that on that same day, I received this anonymous hand-written note through the post. Let me read it – *As righteousness tendeth to life: so he that pursueth evil pursueth it to his own death.* I wonder; do you recognise the writing?"

Richard handed the note to the pastor, who looked at it briefly and handed it back. He faced Richard in as defiant a manner as he could.

"I wrote it. It was sent as a warning to return to the path of righteousness."

Richard stared back at the pastor.

"I have to say, the timing was unfortunate to say the least. You see, we have reason to believe that Colin was murdered by a person or persons associated with your sect. Do you feel that that act of murder represented the path of righteousness?"

"No, no of course not. But why do you suspect one of the Elect? None would do such a thing. I mean who do you suspect?"

"We do not suspect. We know. There was a witness."

"Well – I – I just can't believe one of my flock would commit murder."

"But, Pastor Mutch, this very night you lead a raid on this very place with the intention of burning it to the ground and in the knowledge that, within, there would be people asleep. Had you succeeded, they would almost certainly have died. You yourself incited murder."

"Well I didn't intend – I mean – we – but your people threatened to shoot my members. Yes in fact there were shots. One just missed Billy Smith . . ."

"Any purely defensive use of firearms over the last couple of hours would have been exclusively in the very responsible hands of the Knights of Peace. They came to our aid out of the blue and will depart shortly. Their identities are unknown to us."

Hector resumed the chairman's role at this point and asked if other member of the panel had any further questions. None had. He then addressed the pastor.

"Pastor Erskine Mutch. I think we have now heard enough from you except for one solemn commitment that we seek. But first let me repeat that our foundation is based on principles of peace and tolerance and if I may say – forgiveness. This will remain our touch-stone. However, henceforth, we will also follow the advice of the Romans – *Si vis pacem, para bellum* – If you seek peace, prepare for war.

So this panel, as representative of the Dalmannoch Foundation and its associates seek from you a sworn commitment that you personally and the Elect of the Revelation severally, will never again attack or seek to undermine the Dalmannoch Foundation, its buildings, effects and/or personnel and/or associate groups and their personnel and/or effects. We in turn will not report the events of tonight to the police or other authorities. We will of course retain in safe keeping the bottles, and fingerprints thereon, left behind by your people as a guarantee against any, I trust unlikely, breach of faith.

Do you agree to this Pastor Mutch?"

The pastor swallowed hard.

"I agree."

Hector then held out his hand to shake the trembling hand of Pastor Erskine Mutch.

"Thank you. I'm glad we have come to an accommodation. Our Mr Gordon will draw up a minute of agreement along these lines for you and the Reverend Donald Angus MacLeod to sign on behalf of our respective interests.

While this document is being prepared, perhaps you would like a hot shower and a change of clothes. Brother Richard will show you the way. I'm afraid we do not have the resources to offer the same to all of your members but some hot porridge is being prepared to ease their discomfort."

At that Richard led the bewildered but relieved pastor to the main building.

A NEW DAY

WHILE THE POWWOW had been in progress in the chapel, the Dalmannoch folk had been occupied with a variety of tasks.

Frances, Willie, Suzie and Jonathan were in the kitchen producing porridge, tea and coffee in industrial quantities. The shivering captives were led in relays to the back of the building to the stand pipe outside the kitchen where they were offered the opportunity to wash and to pick up warm food and drink. Frances spoke with several of them to check that there were no serious problems. There were none, other than bruises, cold and generally depressed spirits. The Dalmannoch crew and the Elven Knights were served in the dining room in shifts. Others were occupied with general tidying up.

Gordon Douglas set to work with the chain saw removing the remaining limbs from the fallen tree, after which Sandy McKie's John Deere made light work of lifting the trunk, removing it and the larger branches to the working area at the back of the Dalmannoch main building. There it was stacked to be cut up for fire-wood as fuel for the wood-burning stove and heating system that Gordon had installed. Once that task had been carried out, Gordon, who had earlier sneaked into the bus to disable it by removing the main fuse, now replaced it. The ignition key had been left in situ so Douglas drove the bus up to the Dalmannoch buildings and turned it ready for the eventual departure of the disconsolate members of the fundamentalist sect.

Their departure could not take place until the formality of signing and witnessing of the minute of agreement between the two parties had been carried out. In due course however, Pastor Erskine Mutch emerged, showered, fed and dressed in old overalls borrowed from

Brother Richard. While awaiting the preparation of the document, he talked with members of his flock, ascertaining their condition and thereby assuming something of the pastoral role expected of him.

After a further half hour, Douglas Gordon had drafted and printed copies of the minute of agreement to the satisfaction of Hector. The signatories and witnesses repaired once more to the chapel to complete the formalities. As a final assurance of commitment, a Bible was produced, upon which Pastor Mutch and Hector swore to abide by the terms of the agreement.

With that the members of the Elect of the Revelation boarded their bus and made their exit, surprised no doubt and relieved by the magnanimity of the victors.

Most of the Elven Knights had already departed as had Sandy McKie and his daughter. Those of the defenders that remained foregathered in the common room to be addressed by Hector.

"Well my friends; we have won a decisive victory over those who sought to destroy us. I can but thank you all from the bottom of my heart for rallying to the banner in our hour of need. It has been a long night and I know many of you now have work or other commitments, but before you go let me announce that, in the near future, we will all come together again to celebrate the outcome of what will henceforth be known as the Battle of Dalmannoch Wood. Meanwhile thank you again. Have a safe journey home and God speed."

There was a round of applause, cheers and whoops and then a movement towards cars. As the cars departed, a calm came over Dalmannoch.

Hector looked at his watch. It was still early – just after half past six. He spoke.

"I must go myself with my two colleagues here. I'll be away for a while to meet up with the other members of the order. I'll be back this evening. But, you know, it's a funny thing. When Donald and I were out, rallying the troops, neither of us remembered to contact the police. Probably just as well as things turned out. However, tomorrow we will need to decide what we are going to do about Inspector Huxtable. Interesting, isn't it, that he's a member of the Elect of the Revelation.

* * *

With the departure of Hector, only Richard, Frances and Thomas remained at Dalmannoch and suddenly all was still. Then as a reaction to the efforts and excitement of the previous day and night, a powerful fatigue came over all three. Bed beckoned, if only for a few hours.

Frances was the first to stir. It was eleven o' clock and the sun shone in a clear blue sky. She looked out from the front door to view the scene of recent momentous events. There was now little evidence of the conflict – a flattened patch of grass where the detainees had been corralled and further away a brown patch near the point at which the drive emerged from the wood. From this, a distinct whiff of 'the country' emanated.

She then busied herself in the kitchen, tidying up after the mass production of porridge, tea and coffee. It was almost midday when Richard appeared and another half hour after that before Thomas stuck his head round the kitchen door.

"Is there any chance of something to eat, I'm famished."

"Of course, come and join us," confirmed Frances. I was about to make some brunch – fried bacon, eggs, mushrooms and toast – a bit unhealthy but tasty."

"Excellent, just what I need after yesterday and last night. Some how-do-you-do wasn't it? And some result. I don't think we'll have any more trouble from the Elect."

As the three of them consumed the meal, they recapped the extraordinary battle, filling each other in on details of which the others had been unaware. The conversation then turned to Thomas's own tale, when the phone rang. It had evidently been reconnected. Richard went through to the reception room to answer. It was Professor Macdonald, who had been trying to get through since the previous evening. He was about to depart from Inverness and would arrive at Dalmannoch about evening meal time. Richard very briefly outlined recent events to the great surprise of the academic.

"That was Ruairidh. He'll be here tonight. He can't wait to get the low down on what happened. He wants to meet Duggie first thing – something about the Institute's finances. I didn't mention the fact that you had turned up Thomas, just in case ears were listening."

And so after a quiet afternoon at Dalmannoch, the professor arrived at about seven o' clock, followed a few minutes later by Hector.

It will be no surprise that discussion over the evening meal took the form of re-living the battle and re-stating how Thomas had witnessed Colin's murder and his subsequent flight to Northern Ireland

"Well, what a turn up for the books and I've missed all the fun. And Thomas it's good to see you back and in one piece."

Ruairidh thought for a bit. "We'll need to consider how we tackle Inspector Huxtable."

Everyone nodded and then Hector, who had had no sleep for thirty six hours, stretched his arms and yawned.

"Well as far as I'm concerned, it'll have to wait until tomorrow. I'm bushed, and not as young as I used to be. I'm off to bed. Good night all."

After they each bid Hector a good night's sleep, Ruairidh piped up again:

"By the way Thomas; you don't have any idea what happened to Colin's computer do you ?"

"Yes, yes I do. Colin had it in the pannier bag of his motor bike. I took it with me to Ireland for safe keeping. It's still in my bag upstairs. Would you like me to get it now?"

"That's wonderful. Yes, I certainly would. It may hopefully throw some light on Colin's researches and help the profile of the institute. I need some positive news because there are some puzzling financial irregularities I can't seem to get my head round. I hope Duggie will be able to help unravel the problem tomorrow."

DALMANNOCH'S SECRETARY AND TREASURER, Douglas Gordon arrived at nine o'clock prompt. Ruairidh gave him half an hour to settle in with his routine and then went to his office.

"Duggie, it's good to see you. I heard you had quite a shindig a couple of nights ago. I hope you have recovered."

There was a brief conversation about the confrontation with Pastor Mutch and his flock, then Ruairidh came to the point of his visit.

"The thing is Duggie, I need your help rather urgently. We have some financial problems at the Institute and I can't fathom what's going on. The outflow of cash seems to be greater than it should be, yet I can't quite see how that's happening. The University's Bursar has been on my back to bring in more income, but I couldn't get access to the main account. He's a real pain in the backside, but he's on annual leave this week and I managed to persuade one of the finance people to provide a print-out of the whole caboodle. Could you reconcile this print-out with the Dalmannoch Trust's ledgers, to see if we can find where the trouble lies?"

Douglas gave a little sigh, made the point that he had a lot on his plate, but agreed to put his other work aside to try to resolve this difficulty which he perceived was causing the professor serious anxiety.

"Leave it with me Professor Macdonald and I'll work my way through it to see if I can identify the problem. Let's talk again this afternoon."

Ruairidh then went to Dalmannoch's library to sit down with Colin's laptop to see what it might reveal. The library was a delight to any researcher. It had been shabby and virtually empty when the Dalmannoch Foundation was set up a year before. Since then it had been refurbished and redecorated to the inspired design of Suzie Silver such that it was now a pleasant place equipped with work tables for study and even two nests of easy chairs round a couple of coffee tables. The book shelves had started to fill up, mainly as a result of donations from supporters and spare volumes and papers from the MacPhedran Institute.

Ruairidh booted up the computer and fortunately, if carelessly, Colin had not password protected his files. Of these there were hundreds, probably thousands, listed under over a dozen folders and numerous sub-folders and even sub-sub- folders. To make a start, the professor clicked on to 'Medieval' to reveal a large number of files and sub-folders such as 'Archaeological', 'Ecclesiastical', 'Gaelic', 'Kingship', 'Norse', 'Pictish', and so on. It was going to be a laborious business tracking down that distillation of Colin's research he was going to report to the Institute, only to be frustrated by his death. The identity of the Elven Knights was now known by Ruairidh, but Colin's angle was not, nor were his more refined findings on the link between Christianity and Paganism. It was important for the prestige of the Institute and as a memorial to Colin himself that this documentation be found.

He ploughed on, stopped briefly for a coffee at about half past eleven and continued until lunch time. He ambled through to the Kitchen, glad to give his eyes a rest. Frances indicated that a light snack would be ready directly. Hector was already there having slept until late, taken a leisurely bath and read the *Caledonian*.

"I see there's a lot in today's paper about Crispin Short. It seems that his whole empire has collapsed and he will pretty well loose his shirt. It's real bad for him, but maybe there will be an opportunity to buy Derriedruie.

I guess it depends on whether or not the planning application for this fun-fair caper goes through."

"Let's hope not," commented Ruairidh. "There have been an awful lot of objections as I understand it, thanks to Colin's and Thomas's campaign. By the way, I had never heard of Derrydruie until a few days ago, but it is clearly important to you and the Knights. And tell me about Barhobble, what's the significance there?"

"Well as I told you, Derrydruie was where the Knights were inaugurated. It remained a place for ceremonials and meetings for many centuries. You see the Knights are organised, such that there are three from east Galloway and three from the west with the Grand Master covering the whole territory. The eastern Knights are initiated at Derrydruie and the western Knights at Barhobble. The white stone you found hidden at the altar is used in the initiation ceremony whereby a new Knight swears allegiance to the order. I'm not at liberty to tell you more."

"I wonder how Colin cottoned on to the Order when you have guarded its secrets so carefully."

The professor's conjectures were interrupted first by the arrival of Duggie followed by Richard and Thomas, whereupon lunch was served. The last named pair had been working in the vegetable patch reinstating the strawberry nets and hoeing.

The conversation turned to the important question of how to bring Colin's murderer to justice.

Richard put forward a proposal.

"It seems to me, knowing what we now know, that the only course of action open to us, is to inform the police. We obviously have to circumvent Huxtable. I think the best approach may be for me to have a quiet word first with DI Morrison to see how he thinks it should be handled. The danger is that if we let the cat out of the bag too soon,

Huxtable may well accuse Thomas of the murder. He has already trailed the 'we have not ruled out the possibility of some form of ritualistic killing' scenario, presumably to suggest some Pagan sacrifice."

"Well, admitted Hector, "that seems as good a plan as any. Ideally if the right inducement were provided, it may be possible to get Huxtable to expose his own guilt. Mind you, from what you have said, he's a cool and wily customer. The whole thing would need to be well planned. Anyway see what DI Morrison thinks."

This was agreed.

Lunch over, accountant and professor repaired to Duggie's office.

"I think I may be on to something professor, I need another hour or so. I'll let you know when I'm ready."

Professor Macdonald then made his way back to the Library, to plough once more through Colin's files. His 'My Music' folder contained a wealth of audio files and lyric texts, but nothing that was helpful to Ruairidh. 'My Pictures': nothing helpful. 'Budget' yielded nothing other than an insight into Colin's apparently improving personal finances. He seemed to be careful with his cash. 'Reports' was an interesting folder. It contained files on Colin's conference papers and other, mainly academic papers by Ruairidh and others. Ruairidh recognised most of them, but again nothing earth shatteringly out-of-the-ordinary.

Next he opened a folder named 'AA'. Surely Colin was not an alcoholic. Whatever else was said against Colin, there were never any reports of his being the worse for drink.

Ruairidh opened the folder. It contained several files. One labelled the 'Agnew Bequest'. It listed the entire and substantial collection, including many rare antiquarian volumes bequeathed by the trustees of the late Alexander Agnew's estate. On arrival, the books had been stuck on the shelves unsorted and the manuscripts stored in boxes. Clearly no one had bothered to sort or catalogue them until Colin had taken it upon himself to do so.

As the professor ran through the list and opened a few of the files, he realised that this was an academic gold mine. He clicked on a file 'Elven Knights'. Eureka ! This, it transpired, was a complete history of the order in much more detail than the description outlined by Hector.

As Ruairidh scanned its contents, his heart raced. Then Duggie arrived in the library, somewhat breathless.

"Professor Macdonald. I think I have cracked it. Come to the office and I'll show you. Someone has been siphoning off funds on a regular basis.

Back in Duggie's office, the Dalmannoch Treasurer took the professor through both Dalmannoch Foundation's nominal ledger and the print out from the University's finance department.

"You see, when you compare the two, the monthly rental payments from the University to Dalmannoch Foundation show up against our invoices correctly, but here's the sneaky bit, another payment a couple of weeks later for the same amount each month has been made by the University to what is called 'Dalman Account'. If we can trace the bank account into which it has been paid we can nail the embezzler."

"Well done Duggie ! Thanks a million. That explains why our costs appear to be higher than expected. This is a job for the police."

Ruairidh found Frances in the herb garden.

"Frances; has Richard left yet to meet with DI Morrison?"

"Yes, he left about an hour ago."

"Oh well, I'll need to make a separate trip, but I'll wait until Richard gets back first."

DETECTIVE INSPECTOR MORRISON

AS SOON AS LUNCH WAS OVER, Richard phoned the local police to make an appointment with Detective Inspector Morrison. He was told the inspector was likely to be available about three o'clock at the station.

On the drive to the station, Richard pondered how he would present the delicate matter that one of DI Morrison's own colleagues was Colin's murderer. On entering the building he was met by Sergeant George Watt who was known to Richard, having been closely involved in resolving the case of Alexander Agnew's murder a year earlier under the direction of DI Morrison. Sergeant Watt was proud of his rich Scots tongue and was quite unselfconscious in employing it to address Richard.

"Hoo are ye daein Brither Richard? It's guid tae see ye. I'll tak ye tae see the inspector richt awa."

And so Richard was shown through to an interview room. The Inspector entered a minute or so later.

"Well Brother Richard we meet again. How are things going at Dalmannoch? Big improvements, I hear, since a year ago."

"Yes indeed. We have made good progress with our Foundation and have plans for extending our operation if we can pull the funds together. However, that is not the reason I came to see you. It's a rather delicate and very serious matter on which I wish to seek your advice.

"Seek away Brother Richard. We are indebted to you and your friends for helping us bring the Wilson brothers to justice. I'm pleased to say they are both safely locked up in the Bar L[1]. What can I do for you?"

---

[1] Bar L is slang for the notorious Barlinnie Prison in Glasgow

"Well Inspector, You will no doubt be aware that our colleague Colin McCulloch was murdered at Sweetheart Abbey almost two weeks ago. He was a research fellow working under Professor Ruairidh Macdonald of the MacPhedran Institute of Celtic studies. The institute is based in Inverness but has, what you may call, an outstation at Dalmannoch. That's where Colin was based.

Colin's case is being handled by DI Huxtable at Dumfries and Professor Macdonald and I went to see him last Monday to give him such background information as we could about Colin.

Since then we have come across some very disturbing information. You see, there was a witness to the murder and we have learnt who the murderer was."

The detective inspector, who had a high regard for Brother Richard, was clearly surprised by this statement which, had it come from some stranger, would perhaps have been treated with some scepticism.

"This is a very helpful lead. If you'll tell me who the witness is and who he believes the murderer to be, I'll get on to DI Huxtable right away. He can take the case forward."

Richard held up his hand as a gesture to stop DI Morrison from saying any more

"Unfortunately, I'm afraid it's not that simple Inspector Morrison. You see, the difficulty is that, according to the eye witness, it was DI Huxtable himself who killed Colin. And I have to say that I have absolute confidence in this witness.

The inspector mopped his brow.

"Good God. Let me get this straight. You are saying that our Detective Inspector Alex Huxtable is a murderer."

"I'm sorry Inspector, I know it must come as a shock to you, but I'm afraid that is the case. That's why I have come to you to see how best this information should be handled. You see DI Huxtable had an accomplice on the night of the murder and it is almost certain that one or other of them also killed the young girl from the Craigdoune Childrens' Home – the girl whose body was washed up some days ago. The difficulty is that I believe DI Huxtable will try to pin the murder on the man who witnessed the incident. It's because of this danger that I wanted to seek your advice as to the best way forward."

"Well Brother Richard, this is a very serious accusation. I am going to bring Sergeant Watt to the table so that you can make a full statement."

The inspector absented himself for some five minutes and reappeared accompanied by Sergeant Watt. Richard then reiterated the saga without revealing the identity of Thomas Nutter or the details of his trip to Northern Ireland. When pressed on this, Richard insisted that, because of the danger to the witness, he would not reveal his identity until there was a clear and satisfactory plan for proceeding and some guarantee of the witness's safety.

The inspector was not at all happy with Richard's recalcitrance, but had to accept that until a plan was in place, the identity of the witness would not be forthcoming. He noted, however, Richard's assurance that he and his associates were otherwise more than happy to cooperate actively with the police to bring DI Huxtable and his accomplice to justice.

At the conclusion of the meeting, the inspector indicated that he would discuss the matter with his superiors and that meantime Brother Richard and his associates should hold themselves ready for whatever might transpire over the next few days.

Meanwhile Ruairidh had been busy that afternoon reading through Colin's notes on Alexander Agnew's unique collection. It included collections of local nineteenth century oral tradition on rituals and beliefs that clearly drew on pre-Christian practices. There were more accounts of the Elven Knights activities over the centuries plus folk tales and legends about them. The file that moved the professor most was an incomplete draft of a paper, which Colin had obviously hoped to submit, summarising and analysing this matchless corpus. Had he been able to do so, it would have set Colin on a path to academic celebrity. How sad that this potential had been cut short by his untimely death.

Ruairidh needed to share with someone his excitement at what Colin had uncovered. He called on Hector, who was relaxing in his apartment.

Hector was acutely interested.

"Ruairidh, I'm glad you came to me first, before throwing this open to a wider public. You see, from my standpoint, this is something of a pivotal moment. What Colin stumbled across has been hidden for a long long time – and for good reasons. It was Alexander Agnew's life's work and I must ask you to treat it with the utmost respect. Had it not been for his untimely death last year, I have absolutely no doubt he would have passed his papers about the Order to the Grand Master rather than his executors including them with his wider collection.

Times are changing, however, and perhaps the time has come for the Galloway Knights of Peace to reveal themselves in some way. Monday night's battle was a bit of a turning point. It's a long time since the Knights were out in force as they were on the night of the battle. And we cut rather a dash, didn't we?"

The professor had to concur.

"So I heard."

Hector continued:

"In that action, the cloak of secrecy was removed and I can tell you that already the Order is considering how this new circumstance should be handled. Give us a little time and I hope we may be able to work together, with your institute, to do justice to Colin's, and Alexander Agnew's efforts."

Ruairidh agreed.

At that moment, Richard was heard drawing up at Dalmannoch's front door. Ruairidh and Hector went down to the kitchen to hear about the meeting with DI Morrison. Duggie had gone off to meet a client and was not to return that day, but Frances was already there baking and Thomas had just appeared in the hope of a cup of tea.

As the ex-monk joined them, he described the exchange with the inspector and Sergeant Watt.

Thomas summed up the situation.

"Well, the fat's in the fire now. I hope the police get Huxtable before he gets me."

COLIN'S FUNERAL

TWO WEEKS HAD ELAPSED since Colin and Thomas had set out on that fateful journey which had ended with Colin's murder and Thomas's flight into hiding. The Dumfries police had held on to Colin's body for over a week pending their half-hearted and inconclusive investigations. At last, however, Colin's funeral was scheduled for Thursday at eleven in the funeral parlour of Messrs J McDougall & Sons in Stranraer.

Ruairidh had spoken on the previous afternoon with Mrs McCulloch and with the funeral directors and it was agreed that he would give the obituary to Colin and say something of his significant contribution to the world of academe. Although Colin had been an agnostic, the Reverend Donald Angus MacLeod had also agreed to address the gathering in appropriate terms.

And so it was at a little after nine that Ruairidh, Richard, Frances and Thomas set off for Stranraer in Ruairidh's green Volvo. This was Thomas's first outing beyond Dalmannoch and its immediate policies since he had arrived from Northern Ireland and as a precaution he wore his dark glasses and broad brimmed hat. Hector, Duggie and several of the Gaelic group and of the coven were to make their own way to Stranraer.

A number of attendees were already present in the funeral parlour. Mrs McCulloch was seated at the front with Minerva Skinner, and Colin's history teacher Gus McDougall who, as it happened, was a cousin of the funeral undertakers. Seated near the back of the parlour was Angela Trevelyan, looking uncharacteristically demure in a mauve coat and black trouser suit and cloche hat. Had it not been for the Dalmannoch contingent, however, there would have been very few to mourn Colin's passing.

At the appointed time, the Reverend Donald Angus welcomed those present, made his introductory remarks and announced the opening hymn, which, at Mrs McCulloch's request, was Abide with Me. After a short scripture reading by Duggie, Professor Ruairidh Macdonald gave a glowing eulogy describing the quality of Colin's work and his passion for justice and the tragedy of his young life being cut short when he held such promise. After an invitation to reflect on Colin's life, the Gaelic Group struck up An Innis Aigh, a moving and hopeful Gaelic song from the Gaelic community in Cape Breton Island in the Canadian Province of Nova Scotia.

> Seinn an duan seo dhan Innis Àigh,
> An innis uaine as gile tràigh;
> Bidh sian air uairean a' bagairt cruaidh ris
> Ach 's e mo luaidh-sa bhith ann a' tàmh.

Guitar arpeggio accompaniment was provided by Iain Stewart.

The funeral service ended with a minute of silent reflection, and closing words by The Reverend Donald Angus.

The coffin was duly transferred to the hearse and the cortege moved *en convoy* to Gallowhill Road, to the South-West of Stranraer for the interment at the Glebe Cemetery. Among the pallbearers were Hector, Richard, Ruairidh and Thomas. Once more a few words from the Reverend Donald Angus and, as the coffin was lowered, the unusual and adaptable minister took up his pipes and played Flowers of the Forest and ended with Flower of Scotland, for Colin had been a fervent Scottish Nationalist, as, in point of fact, albeit discretely, was Donald Angus himself.

Standing a little to the rear of the group, observing the proceedings was Detective Inspector Alexander Huxtable.

It was Richard who noticed him first and he spoke discretely to Ruairidh and Thomas.

"Don't turn round, but DI Huxtable is watching us. He's about fifteen yards behind you. Don't let him see you have noticed. And Thomas you'd better, slowly, put your hat back on."

Thomas had removed his hat during the interment as a token of respect. As casually as he could, he replaced it on his head and hoped that the beard and dark glasses would have been sufficient to conceal his identity from the detective.

People started to drift away, as did Thomas, flanked by Richard and Ruairidh. They carefully avoided eye contact with Inspector Huxtable as they made to depart from the cemetery. Just before they reached the gate, Angela Trevelyan came over to address Ruairidh.

"Professor Macdonald, I don't know if you remember me. I attended a couple of your conferences at Dalmannoch. Such a tragic business. Poor Colin. Who would have thought this would have happened."

"Ah yes, Angela, indeed I do remember you. It's very good of you to come all this way to pay your respects".

"Well, it's the least I could do. You see Colin and I were – em – very close, until – well, until my husband felt we were too close. But what I wanted to say was that Colin confided a lot in me and used me as a sounding board for trying out his research findings. He had unearthed some very interesting material and I just feel it would be a shame if his work were to go unrecognised. The thing is; I wondered if you might let me help pull it together as a posthumous memorial to Colin."

The professor was somewhat surprised by the offer, not least by the time and place in which it was made. He was, however, intrigued by its possibilities.

"Hmm, Angela, I think this may be something we could discuss, but I rather think not here. Mrs McCulloch has arranged for sandwiches at the Swan Inn in Seuchan Street. We are going to call in for a few minutes, just to thank Mrs McCulloch and then we're heading back to Dalmannoch. Why don't you come round this evening and we can talk about it then."

This was agreed.

As the little group left the cemetery, Richard noticed with some unease that DI Huxtable was speaking with some of the other departing mourners. Had he rumbled the identity of Thomas? For the present Richard kept his fears to himself.

The visit to the Swan Inn was a brief one, just long enough for a sandwich, a cup of tea and to have a few sympathetic words with Mrs McCulloch, Minerva and a few others before heading off to Dalmannoch. In fact several of the mourners had taken their leave directly from the cemetery to resume work or domestic commitments.

On the way to Dalmannoch, Ruairidh stopped the car round the corner from the police station to report the fraudulent withdrawal of funds from the institute's accounts as discovered by Duggie. It was Sergeant Watt who attended to him.

"Wiel, this is a serious matter richt enyuch. I'll tak a note o it, but it's really for the Highland Police tae sort oot, sin the fraud seems to be perpetrated there. Ye should let them ken as soon as ye can."

The professor acknowledged that this was a sound suggestion and agreed that he would phone the police in Inverness directly. As he was about to leave the police station, DI Morrison appeared.

"Ah Professor Macdonald, perhaps you can help me. I believe you know Thomas Nutter who is a member of a Pagan group that meets from time to time at Dalmannoch."

"Yes I know him. What can I do for you ?"

"A warrant is being made out for his arrest for the murder of Colin McCulloch. Do you know his whereabouts?"

The professor was quite taken aback by this announcement. He sought to play for time.

"Surely Mr Nutter is innocent of such an act. However, I can tell you that he lives at Elven Cottage, just outside Wigtown."

"We have just checked, and he is not at home."

Ruairidh shrugged and opined:

"I suppose he must have gone out. Now if you'll excuse me, I have an appointment with an academic colleague and am in danger of running late."

With that the professor left the police station, made his way back to the car and related what had just transpired to Richard, Frances and Thomas.

"Well I'll be damned," exploded Richard with uncharacteristically strong language, "After me explaining the true circumstances to Morrison. Huxtable must have spotted you at the interment Thomas and set wheels in motion. Let's get out of here. We need to take evasive action – and quick!

OBFUSCATION

BY THE TIME Richard, Frances, Ruairidh and Thomas returned to Dalmannoch, it was about three o' clock. The mood among them was sombre indignation and, in Thomas's case, fury at the injustice of his situation.

"I might have known this would happen when I came back. First the bastard tries to kill me, now he frames *me* for the murder he committed."

Scarcely had they crossed the threshold when Hector's Land Rover scrunched to a halt in the drive way. He joined them in the kitchen where Frances had put on the inevitable kettle.

Once Hector learned of the unexpected turn of events, over a coffee, he took charge of the situation.

"OK. First; you can bet your bottom dollar the cops will be here before long sniffing around and looking for Thomas. Second; Thomas, we better get you the Hell out of here into a safe hiding place. Third; we need to set a trap for that bastard Huxtable – and you Thomas, I'm afraid will be the bait."

The others listened and nodded admiringly at Hector's clear-headed decisiveness and, by that token, understood the reason for his success in business. He continued:

"Now Thomas, you go and pack an overnight bag and I'll phone my cousin."

Thomas sprinted up to his room and Hector made his way to the office. He lifted the receiver; the dialling tone had been restored. He started to dial, and then stopped. What was that faint click? Was the phone tapped? He replaced the receiver and returned to the kitchen.

"Guys; I think there may be a tap on the phone. Best not use it for any but the most routine calls. I'll take

Thomas with me and I'll report back when we have secured a safe house."

Richard then spoke up.

"Look; Thomas needs back up and probably a witness when whatever happens with Huxtable, happens. I'll come with him. Just let me gather up my overnight gear."

Hector assented, but Frances displayed some anxiety and she wrapped her arms around Richard.

"Oh my love, I know you want to help Thomas, but please be careful. I worry about you."

The ex-monk responded with a hug and:

"Don't worry my darling Frances. I'll be fine and so will Thomas. You'll see".

Frances gave Richard a loving kiss, then he disappeared upstairs. A couple of minutes later he and Thomas reappeared ready to depart. Before they did so, Hector offered some words of advice as to how Frances and Ruairidh should handle and seek to confuse the anticipated police enquiries. He went up to his own quarters to come back with a small black equipment bag.

"OK, let's hit the road before the cops turn up."

And with that Hector drove off with his two passengers. Where, Frances and Ruairidh knew not.

Barely ten minutes had elapsed before the predicted police car materialised just outside the front door of Dalmannoch's main building. The door bell sounded and Ruairidh stood in the kitchen quietly reciting a line from a vintage television programme[1]:

"One, two, three, four – keep them waiting at the door;

Five, six, seven, eight – it always pays to make them wait;

---

[1] CJ in the The Fall and Rise of Reginald Perrin

173

Nine, ten – come!"

At this signal Frances, who had in her youth thought to pursue an acting career, opened the door and with a broad and welcoming smile and a mildly quizzical look, addressed the two men standing before her.

"Good afternoon gentlemen. What can I do for you ?"

Straight-faced, one of the 'gentlemen' pulled a warrant card from his pocket and waved it in front of Frances.

"I'm Detective Inspector Huxtable. I'm looking for Thomas Nutter."

Frances inspected the warrant card carefully and feigning mild surprise and ignorance smiled.

"Oh, I see. You're detectives. Fancy that. That'll be why you're not wearing uniforms. Well I'm afraid you've come to the wrong place. Mr Nutter lives at Elven Cottage just outside Wigtown. You should find him there. I hope he's not in any trouble. He's such a nice man."

Clearly this did not go down well with the detective inspector, but he tried not to show his irritation.

"We have already called there and there was no response. We have reason to believe he may be here. We need him to help with our enquiries about the murder of Colin McCulloch."

"Poor Colin. I have just come back from his funeral – such a gifted academic; so they say. I certainly hope you catch whoever was responsible for his cruel death and lock them up for a very long time. I'm sure Mr Nutter will be happy to help with that in any way he can."

With a serious, but encouraging demeanour, Frances made to withdraw.

"Well Mr Hutchison it was nice talking to you. I hope the perpetrator of this terrible crime is brought to justice."

"The name is Huxtable, Detective Inspector Huxtable. You say Thomas Nutter is not here. When did you last see him?"

"Forgive me Mr Hu – Huxtable, is it? Yes now, when did I see him? Let me think now. Sure, he was here on Monday night with a bunch of our friends – here at Dalmannoch. We had some trouble with some nasty hooligans. Crazy Religious fanatics they were. The boys here sorted them out. Just a combination of firmness and forgiveness – a lesson in what Christianity should be about, don't you think?"

Frances well knew that, as a member of the Elect of the Revelation, DI Huxtable would very quickly have been informed about 'the battle' and would doubtless not have agreed with the interpretation of Christianity just outlined. She also quickly realised that the inspector would have seen Thomas in her, Richard's and Ruairidh's company.

"Oh and I've just remembered, silly me. He was at the funeral of Colin McCulloch this very morning. After it was over the mourners went their various ways and here I am. And here Mr Nutter is not," she gave a little girlish giggle. "I hope that has been helpful to you."

DI Huxtable was beginning to show his irritation.

"No. I don't think it takes us much further forward. Your name is . . ?

"Frances".

"Frances . . ?"

"Yes Frances".

"Frances what?"

"Ah – McGarrigle".

"I understand a Brother Richard Wells lives here."

"Yes; that's right. He's my lover."

The inspector went slightly red in the face at this brazen admission, but recovered quickly.

"I'd like to speak to him."

"Sure you and me both," retorted Frances in her best Donegal accent with a wink and knowing smile.

"What do you mean by that?"

"Oh he went off on one of his walkabouts. He's a former monk you know. He likes a bit of solitude now and then to contemplate his God. He was very upset by Colin's murder. He's not a vengeful man, but I suspect he is praying for God's judgement on the murderer."

"When will he be back?"

"Oh, that is a good question Mr Hux . . . What's your name again?"

"Detective Inspector Huxtable."

The inspector emphasised the 'Detective Inspector' appellation.

"Ah yes, Mr Huxtable. Who knows when he'll be back ? But when he does come back, the first thing I'm going to do is take him up to bed for a good shag. After that I'll tell him you were looking for him."

The inspector had heard enough. Without a further word, he turned around and urged his silent, but slightly smirking colleague back to the police car, which departed in a spray of gravel.

Frances stood in the doorway watching the car disappear down the drive and into the woodland. She was joined by Ruairidh.

"Well done Frances. You played that beautifully – worthy of an Oscar. I don't know how you kept a straight face. The man must be absolutely livid. You've undermined just about everything he stands for. I love it.

How about a gin and tonic before Angela arrives?"

A couple of folding chairs were brought out to the lawn. As they sipped their drinks, Frances pondered:

"I wonder where Richard and Thomas are?"

THE TRAP IS SET

FOR THE FIRST FEW MILES, Hector took the Land Rover by a series of back roads to reduce the possibility of meeting a police car. None was encountered and, after a bit, he regained the main highway network and headed with his passengers for his cousin's place at Glenshillan. A mile or so before reaching the house, he stopped.

"You two had better get out here for half an hour or so to admire the view. The less my good kinfolks know the less they can tell."

Richard and Thomas alighted. Hector then drove up to Glenshillan House and rang the front door bell. Hilda, his cousin's wife answered.

"Hector, how lovely. I thought I heard a car." Hector gave Hilda a little peck on the cheek. "Come in, come in. James is out on the hill, but he'll be back before dinner. You'll stay to eat with us of course."

"Thanks Hilda, but no, not on this occasion. I'm in a bit of a rush. It was you I wanted to see as a matter of fact."

James and Hilda were an enterprising couple who managed their estate efficiently with an eye to profitable new activities. Besides the shooting and fishing, Hector was aware that his relations had refurbished a number of redundant estate cottages and outbuildings as comfortable holiday accommodation. To supplement this successful part of their business, they had also recently bought and renovated a couple of small properties, in pleasant locations off the estate. It was in the light of this that Hector broached his proposition.

"I have a couple of friends, looking for a quiet place to stay for a couple of nights. I just wondered if one of your cottages might be free. I'll cover the bill of course."

"Well you know Hector, we're getting into the busy season now, but I think you may be in luck. Let's check the book."

Hilda ushered Hector to a little office at the back of the house and opened a large dog eared note book.

"Let me see. Ah yes, I though so. We had a cancellation at Seaview Cottage, down on the Colvend Coast. It's available until Saturday morning. Would that do?"

Hector readily agreed, attended to the necessary formalities there and then, made his excuses and drove back to where he had left Richard and Thomas.

Thomas was sitting on a stone, looking somewhat dejected. Richard was standing admiring the view over a large swath of Galloway.

"OK you guys, I've got you a billet for the next few nights if needs be. With luck we'll bring this whole darned business to an end within the next twenty four hours."

Thomas's mood remained gloomy.

"All I can say is, I hope the 'end' doesn't mean me spending the rest of my life in the nick for a murder I didn't commit."

"Don't worry old son," Hector cajoled, "It'll work out all right. Have a little faith. As far as I'm concerned, the only one heading for the pen is Detective Inspector Huxtable."

The trio set off for the coast, calling on the way at Dalbeattie for supplies to make an evening meal and breakfast.

The Colvend and Southwick shore is a particularly scenic area much favoured in the past by Manx smugglers and today by walkers and birdwatchers. Seaview Cottage was located up a side road and, true to its name, it had spectacular views over the Solway Firth and the Cumbrian Fells. There were a number of other dwellings or holiday homes in the vicinity, but none was visible from the cottage itself, which was small, but cheerfully decorated, with two bedrooms, a bathroom and an open-plan kitchen cum lounge.

After a quick inspection of the interior and the surrounding grassed area, there was agreement that Seaview Cottage would serve as a satisfactory hide away. The back door opened onto a kind of patio equipped with a deal table and benches. It was round this table that the three men sat to ponder the future.

The business mind of Hector had been quietly working away since he had been told earlier that afternoon of the police intention to arrest Thomas. He now gave voice to his thoughts.

"What we have to do is to turn the tables on Huxtable. I won't deny there are risks – big risks, but I bet Huxtable is feeling just as vulnerable as you are Thomas. Unlike you two, I haven't met the man, but from the soundings I have made among the Knights, he has strengths and weaknesses. We must try to neutralise his strengths and exploit his weaknesses. He's clearly cunning and ruthless and has the resources of the constabulary to aid him, but his extreme and unattainable religious standards must inevitably undermine his self-belief. Our trump card is: we have truth on our side and he knows it."

Thomas, who had everything to lose if things went wrong, listened intently. He was by no means convinced at the chances of success.

"That's all very well, but how do we get the evidence that he is Colin's killer. Without that it's his word against mine. If he can, he'll kill me and if he can't, he'll get me life for murder. Neither outcome has much attraction for me. Remember he had an accomplice. They've probably already concocted some trumped-up story to condemn me."

Hector nodded.

"You are right Thomas. You are in very dangerous waters, but there is a way. We must entice Huxtable here, alone, and get him to condemn himself with his own words."

"How on earth do we do that?"

Hector held up the black equipment bag that he had picked up from his apartment at Dalmannoch. He tapped it with his finger and gestured:

"Let's go inside and I'll explain."

Thomas and Richard followed Hector into the cottage. He placed the bag on the kitchen table. He opened it to reveal a small CCTV camera, microphone, and laptop computer.

"With this, we should be able to gather incontrovertible evidence. We'll need to stage a little performance and you guys will be the actors. I'm glad Richard that you have come along. You and Thomas will be the double act we need to throw Huxtable off balance. That will allow me to hang back in reserve."

As Hector outlined his plan, he set up the camera and mike so as to capture most of what might transpire in the room. The laptop was located in the bedroom that was to be occupied by Thomas. Instruction was given on the operation of the device, after which Hector took his leave. He promised to return in the morning before the plan of action was launched.

Thomas and Richard now had the place to themselves. They both suddenly felt very hungry. The supplies were broached and a meal prepared. There was little appetite for conversation as the meal was consumed. Before turning in for the night, the pair went out for a walk along the cliff top to stretch their legs and fill their lungs with sea air. The dangers of the morrow, however, clouded both of their minds such that the exercise and the views did little to raise their spirits.

On retiring, when sleep came, in both cases, it was fitful and laced with unpleasant dreams.

NUALA

BACK AT DALMANNOCH after dinner that evening Angela Trevelyan called and Ruairidh discussed with her the possibility of her assisting in taking forward aspects of Colin's researches. After that short meeting she departed.

With nothing else to occupy them, Frances and Ruairidh sat by the fire in the common room waiting for Hector's return. Time seemed to pass interminably slowly. Ruairidh looked at Frances as she sat there self-contained, strong but justifiably anxious. He sought to relieve their joint gloom.

"I'm glad you and Richard have found so much happiness here at Dalmannoch. You are so well matched, the pair of you. It's a damned shame this business has cast such a shadow over the place."

"I know. I love Richard more than I can say. And I'm in no doubt he loves me with a powerful love. It frightens me sometimes – if anything should . . ."

"Richard will be just fine." The professor did his best to hide his own anxiety and sought to reassure. "You know he can handle himself – despite that gentle demeanor, he's as tough as old boots."

"Oh I know that – but . . ."

"Look, we can't do anything just now. There's no point in dwelling on what ifs. Why don't you tell me about your life in Ireland before you came this side of the water? You know I have Irish blood in my veins too."

"Really? I didn't know that." Frances eyes brightened. "How is that?"

"I'll tell you once you tell me about your own cinneadh[1]. You go first."

---

[1] Cinneadh a Gaelic word meaning kin, ancestry

And so Frances described her happy childhood in Letterkenny, County Donegal, with her late school teacher father, Sean McGarrigle and her Gaelic speaking mother Nuala, an O'Brien from Gweedore on the far western seaboard. She described the wonderful summer holidays at Gweedore when, as children, she and her brother Finbarr ran wild and free in that rugged and seductive land with the numerous Gaelic speaking offspring of their equally numerous Gaelic speaking relations.

Frances' father had married her mother when he had been in his forties and she fifteen years younger. He had died some years ago aged seventy one of an aneurism. Her late father's older, somewhat eccentric unmarried sister, Mary McGarrigle, a former music teacher, and Frances' favourite aunt, had died in Bristol not two years before. It was she who left Frances and Finbarr a considerable inheritance from which Frances had been able to invest in Dalmannoch.

Frances' brother Finbarr was a successful Dublin accountant with a firm specialising in company insolvencies and liquidations. He and his girl-friend Imelda lived in Portmarnock, an affluent Dublin dormitory settlement. Since moving to Dalmannoch a year before, Frances had, on a couple of occasions, availed herself of Irish ferry services from nearby Cairnryan to visit Finbarr in the south and her mother at Letterkenny in the west. Both had promised to come to visit Dalmannoch to see for themselves Frances' much enthused about new home, but had not so far done so.

Ruairidh was pleased to see Frances relax as she described her Irish roots.

"Your mother's name is Nuala," Ruairidh observed. "That was my grandmother's name."

"Ah, ha; so that is where your Irish blood comes from ?"

"Yes. Her name was Nuala Kierley – Nuala O'Carroll as she originally was, for she was married before she met my grandfather."

At this, Frances seemed to show a special curiosity. She paused in thought, then:

"Mm – interesting – Kierley – O'Carroll. How did they meet – your grandfather and this Nuala Kierley?"

"Well you see," the professor expounded; "My grandfather, Archie MacDonald, was a captain in the Seaforth Highlanders. As a Gael of the old school, and an inveterate fisherman, he loved Ireland and had a number of good friends in the Emerald Isle, especially upland farmer, ex Edinburgh University pal called Sean Glynn – a dyed-in-the-wool republican. Grandfather found himself in the south west of Ireland in 1920 and 21 in charge of a British garrison in a place called Castletown. That was during the Black and Tan War. Although he despised the brutality of the Tans, he was, nonetheless, now technically an enemy of his Irish friends. Through a strange turn of events Captain MacDonald and his sister, my Great Aunt Margaid, were apprehended by an IRA Flying Column while on a fishing expedition. Such was the mutual respect between insurgents and Highlanders that they were held under a rather pleasant house arrest until the truce was agreed between the British and the Irish, pending the drafting of the peace treaty. For seven weeks they were thus in rebel hands.

As it happened, his old friend Sean Glynn was the intelligence officer and main link between the Flying Column and IRA HQ in Dublin. It was there too that my grandfather caught a first brief sight of Nuala Kierley in the light of the turf fire. In those few seconds, he was captivated by her beauty. She, an Irish patriot to the core, had played a key part in uncovering a traitor to the cause. The traitor was none other than her own husband Martin.

Sean had escorted Nuala from Dublin to the safety of the south west and from there, who knew where? The traitor was captured and a week later, on the very night of the truce, Martin Kierley escaped and was found next morning, drowned.

In seven years nothing was seen or heard of Nuala Kierley either by my grandfather or any of the men of the former Flying Column.

Then, in 1928, retired now as Major Archibald MacDonald, he caught the Burns and Laird steamer from Glasgow to Dublin to meet up again with Sean Glynn for a month's fishing in Ireland's south west. As he strolled round the once familiar Dublin streets to reacquaint himself with the, now peaceful, capital of the Irish Free State, he chanced across, and fell into conversation with, a blond woman of striking beauty. On being hailed by a man, however, whom she called Harry, she made off alone by tram, but not before referring to my grandfather as Captain MacDonald.

Puzzled, the ex-soldier went back to the hotel where he had arranged to meet Sean Glynn – and then the penny dropped. The blond woman was none other than Nuala Kierley.

The man, Harry, or Sir Henry Hanley was a wealthy English impresario and ex-British agent who it transpired intended to marry Nuala – an unwise move in the opinion of Sean, and Sean was her cousin. That same night after a theatre performance Sean and the major abducted Nuala from under the wrathful guard of Hanley. They would have preferred the term "rescued". They took her to Kerry to the tranquil farm of ex Flying Column member, Paddy Bawn Enright, where she was able to recover from the traumas and uncertainties of her previous seven years of exile. It was during this period that my grandfather, hitherto a confirmed bachelor, fell deeply in love with Nuala and after a final tussle with Sir Henry, the match was sealed.

Grandfather and Nuala married in 1930. They set up home, and a happy home it was, in the Highlands. Of course they made periodic visits to Ireland, Sean and the "boys" of the Flying Column. My father was born in 1932 and so here am I.

It's a romantic story, isn't it?"

Frances had listened with wrapt attention to this tale of war and love and the rebirth of her motherland.

"It *is* romantic, but I can tell you something you don't know oh wise and omniscient Professor Ruairidh Alasdair Macdonald. My father's mother was an O'Carroll and a second cousin of both Nuala Kierley and Sean Glynn. I remember as a child, Daddy talking of Nuala, Sean, Paddy and the others of the Flying Column and how Nuala married a Scots Army officer. In fact there was a book written about their exploits.[1] So, you see, it seems that you and I are distant blood cousins.

My mother will love to meet you when she comes over to Dalmannoch."

---

[1] *Green Rushes* by Maurice Walsh, also published as *The Quiet Man and Other Stories*

HUXTABLE TAKES THE BAIT

ABOUT TEN THE NEXT MORNING Hector reappeared at Seaview Cottage. Richard and Thomas had risen early, had breakfasted and tidied up. They were anxious to hear what further plans Hector had for unmasking DI Huxtable and for clearing Thomas's name.

"Well it was pretty late by the time I got back to Dalmannoch last night. I had some business to attend to. But, according to Ruairidh, Frances had a bit of fun with Huxtable, winding him up and hopefully putting him off his stride a bit. Anything that can disorientate him is valuable. This morning one of my colleagues should have put in an anonymous call to Huxtable from a phone box to say that you, Thomas, were spotted at Newton Stewart, so that should keep them busy on a wild goose chase for a while. Frances told me that Huxtable wanted to speak with you Richard; presumably to see how much you know. She told him you had gone on a sort of spiritual retreat. That is just the ticket because you, Richard, are now the bait to bring Huxtable here."

Richard was not overjoyed with being bait and sought clarification.

For the rest of the morning, I suggest you pair go for a good walk to enjoy the views and clear your heads, find a café and have a bite of lunch. Then you, Thomas, should get back to the cottage, hide yourself in your bedroom and be ready to switch on the surveillance equipment. You, Richard, should go to a call box, ring Huxtable (here's his number)," Hector handed Richard a slip of paper. "You should then tell him that you have been walking, but got the message that he was looking for you. You then arrange to meet him at Seaview Cottage, but insist that you want to see him alone, otherwise you won't turn up and he'll have to wait till you get back to Dalmannoch. Then phone my mobile (the number is on the paper I gave you) and let me know the agreed appointment time.

Make your way back to the cottage in good time for his arrival. From then you play it by ear, but try to find out what evidence Huxtable has concocted to implicate Thomas."

There were a few questions from both Thomas and Richard on points about which they wished to be absolutely clear. The course of action was agreed, Hector departed and the remaining pair shut the cottage door behind them and strode out somewhat more purposefully than they had the night before. As directed, they had lunch, Thomas returned to the cottage and Richard made his calls. It was just before three o clock when Richard returned to Seaview Cottage. He checked that Thomas was in post. He was and had been in his room for a while, ready to switch on the laptop in good time for the arrival of the detective inspector. He had taken the precaution of drawing the curtains, just in case Huxtable or anyone with him might try to peep in.

Four o clock was the time agreed for DI Huxtable's visit and there was little either Richard or Thomas could do to pass the time. Richard tried to read one of the books provided for the entertainment of cottage users, but he couldn't concentrate. Then at about quarter to four, Thomas switched on the laptop and, as a test, asked Richard to perform and speak to camera and mike. This action was carried out not a minute too soon for the sound of a car drawing up announced the arrival of the inspector. Each man went to his action stations. Thomas in his room with the recording equipment and the door closed and Richard sitting reading his book.

There was a loud knock at the door.

Richard rose and opened the door.

"Good afternoon Inspector. Come in. Come in to my little retreat. Now, how can I help you?"

"I have a warrant for the arrest of Thomas Nutter. When did you last see him?"

"Thomas ? Oh quite recently. He was at the funeral of Colin McCulloch yesterday. But what has he done? Thomas is such a law abiding citizen.

"We intend to arrest him for the murder of Colin McCulloch.

Richard feigned great surprise.

"No – no, I can't believe that. Not Thomas. I'm absolutely sure you're mistaken. What evidence do you have that Thomas would do such a thing?"

DI Huxtable was not used to having his word challenged and began to show irritation.

"This is a serious matter Brother Richard, I'm not obliged to tell you or anyone else what grounds we have for making arrests until the matter goes to court. My job is to find and arrest Thomas Nutter.

"Well Inspector, you can hardly expect me to help you arrest an innocent man when I know of a person who witnessed the murder, and I can tell you that the murderer was not Thomas Nutter. Furthermore; this person witnessed that night, the rape and abduction of a young girl – a girl who was later found cast up dead on the shore. Two men were involved in these heinous crimes and neither one was Thomas Nutter."

The inspector was angered by this turn of events. He raised his voice.

"This is preposterous. Who is this so called witness? We – we have a witness that will testify to the contrary. He will testify that it was Thomas Nutter who murdered Colin McCulloch."

As the inspector blurted out these words, the bedroom door was pulled open and Thomas appeared, pointing at the inspector.

"Then he's a damned liar and you know it Huxtable. Who is this witness? Your rapist accomplice on the night *you* killed Colin. I saw the whole thing. You knifed Colin in cold blood. And you would have killed me too, if I hadn't got away. I bet that spooked you. And that poor girl – where did you dump her body? Look at you, a supposed Christian – a member of the oh-so-pious Elect of the Revelation – you should burn in the Hell you love to condemn others to. Come on. Come on. Tell me to my face that I killed Colin, you hypocrite – you pervert – you murderer."

The inspector's face blanched. He stood for a few seconds open mouthed, and then backing towards the front door, he guffawed:

"You pathetic interfering heathen, you Pagan; you and your Papist friend here won't live to tell what happened that night. I should have killed you there and then, but it's not too late, oh no, it's not too late."

DI Huxtable slipped out of the door followed by Thomas and Richard. There confronting them were the large forms of Bulldog Billy Smith, Sammy (the Sadist) Black and a smaller man, who Thomas recognised as Huxtable's accomplice at Sweetheart Abbey. The trio were now supplemented by Huxtable himself who smirked:

"You see I brought reinforcements. I'm afraid your bodies will be found at the bottom of the cliffs – a sad misadventure".

He then addressed the two ex URHS men.

"OK lads. You know what to do. Grab them.

Billy Smith made a lunge for Richard and Sammy Black made for Thomas. Richard who in his youth had been a boxer swerved Billy's first thrust and landed a good punch on Billy's substantial stomach. Billy, angered, swung at Richard, missed but swung again and caught Richard a glancing blow on the chest and so the two sparred, neither man getting the upper hand.

Meanwhile Sammy and Thomas were engaged in a dirty fight. Thomas's marine training stood him in good stead and Sammy was coming off worse. Out of the corner of his eye, Richard saw Huxtable wield a large club which he aimed at Thomas's legs. Thomas fell. Sammy, the smaller man and Huxtable were on top of him. Thomas struggled to shake them off.

As this transpired, Richard managed to land a right on Billy's jaw followed by a left. Billy staggered backwards dazed and Richard got in another right which sent Billy to the ground. Richard then, in an effort to save Thomas, was about to pull Sammy off the struggling ex-marine. As he did so he heard a strange hooting sound. Then a thwack – he was knocked out by Huxtable's club.

KNIGHTS ERRANT

ECTOR WOODROW-DOUGLAS knew that time was short. He returned first to Dalmannoch to pick up his knightly garb. He felt it unwise to worry Frances with details of what was undoubtedly a risky venture. He took Professor Macdonald aside, however, to update him on events. The professor was keen to be involved in action that would hopefully bring some closure to the murder of his research fellow.

"Look Hector, an extra pair of hands may be useful. I'd like to come along with you."

Hector agreed. The grey Land Rover Discovery was loaded with Hector's gear and the pair set off towards the point of rendezvous with the other members of the Order of the Galloway Knights of Peace. That place, not far from New Galloway, was Gowanbrae, the country seat of one Sir Graham Maxwell, a highly respectable retired lawyer. Sir Graham was elderly, and it is speculated, may formerly have been an active member of the Order. At any rate, it seemed to Ruairidh that he must have been very much in their confidence.

When the Land Rover arrived, there were several other cars parked by the stables towards the rear of the house. Among them was the silver grey Lexus saloon that had transported a number of the knights to Dalmannoch on the eve of the battle. As Hector alighted, carrying a large hold-all, he asked Ruairidh to remain in the car.

"The Knights are shy of having their identities revealed, even to trusted friends like you. I won't be more than twenty minutes or so."

True to his word, seven Elven Knights emerged from the rear of the house, clad as they had been a few nights before – tan riding boots, green mantle charged with the silver Elven Star, balaclava and helmet and each as before bearing a mahogany baton.

Five of them walked to the Lexus; the other two made for the Land Rover. One of these was Hector. The other carried a hunting horn, the very instrument that had so recently signalled the counter attack at Dalmannoch.

"Ruairidh, allow me to introduce Chevalier Ronald. We do not use surnames in the Order," then turning to the said knight, "and this is my good friend Professor Ruairidh Alasdair Macdonald about whom I have already spoken".

The two men shook hands and Hector turned the Land Rover's ignition key, engaged gear and set off for the Colvend Coast, followed by the Lexus. The convoy followed the A 713 down the long east bank of Loch Ken to Castle Douglas. From thence they travelled via the A 745 through Dalbeattie and on to the A 710. A little before the Kippford turn-off they came to a halt at a tail back of traffic. Ruairidh got out and walked a little way up the line of vehicles to ascertain what was causing the hold-up. A driver who was standing by his car, smoking a cigarette, told him the bad news that a timber lorry had shed its load, blocking the highway. It would be hours before it was cleared. Ruairidh hurried back to the Land Rover to inform Hector.

"Dammit. We'll need to turn round and take the Cloak Moss road."

Ruairidh ran back to the Lexus to inform its occupants. The two vehicles performed five point turns, Ruairidh re-joined the Land Rover and they set off again in the opposite direction, back to Dalbeattie. The driver of the Lexus allowed Hector to overtake to regain lead vehicle position. Hector was concerned.

"That's added at least twenty minutes to our journey. I just hope Huxtable doesn't turn up early."

Back at Dalbeattie, the two cars took the A 745 for a couple of miles and then turned right on to the minor road for Sandyhills. Just after the junction they had to slow again. A tractor and wide trailer trundled ahead of them moving at fifteen miles an hour. It was impossible to overtake on the narrow road.

"Holy cow!" The normally unruffled Hector was becoming agitated. "We're never going to get to Seaview Cottage at this rate."

He sounded the land Rover's horn, but the tractor driver seemed to pay no notice.

"Praap, praap, praaaaap" again, but the tractor chugged on regardless, seemingly unconcerned.

Hector was about to explode.

Fortunately, after a further mile the tractor turned off up a farm track and the convoy accelerated once more. In a few minutes they were back on the A 710 and then on to the by-way that led to Seaview Cottage.

As the two cars screeched to a halt, the occupants could see that the unequal melee outside the cottage had reached the stage at which Thomas had been felled and Richard had delivered Billy Smith a knock-out blow.

The Elven Knights quickly alighted from their vehicles. As they did so, Hector saw Huxtable take aim at Richard's head with his club. Chevalier Ronald blew the hunting horn, but it was too late to prevent Huxtable dealing Richard a serious blow.

The Knights and Professor Macdonald charged towards the cottage. Huxtable and his cronies looked up and then in panic started to scatter at the sight of the fantastical cloaken figures. The two ex URHS men, already bruised and exhausted from their exertions were immediately nabbed, as was their smaller companion.

Huxtable, who had a few seconds head start, made off in a seaward direction pursued by two of the Elven

Knights. He was clearly very fit and boosted by adrenalin. He raced ahead along the top of the cliff. He turned round briefly to judge the proximity of his pursuers. In so doing, he lost his footing, staggered backwards, clawed the air trying to right himself, but slipped over the edge of the cliff. He managed to grasp on to a narrow grassy ledge. Breathless, the two knights approached him. One anchored himself against a rock and the other holding the first knights left hand, offered his right to Huxtable who was dangling over a sheer drop.

Whether the cornered inspector simply lost his grip, or decided to end his own life, is not clear, but as his fingers slowly opened. The watching knights saw on his face a strange grimace – a smile almost, and then as Huxtable's fingers lost their purchase on the ledge, he fell without a sound to certain death.

The two knights peered over the cliff edge to see the battered body of DI Huxtable impaled lifeless on the jagged rocks far below. There was nothing more they could have done to save him.

By the time they had returned to the cottage to report the fall of DI Huxtable, Billy Smith and Sammy Black were already tied and seated back to back cursing their green cloaked captors. The other man, who in the event had put up little fight, was also bound and presented for inspection. Ruairidh looked at him; he looked again in astonishment.

"Winkley? Howard Winkley what the Hell are you doing here?"

Howard Winkley said nothing.

AFTERMATH

ONCE THE DUST HAD SETTLED, the most immediate concern of Hector and Ruairidh was the condition of Brother Richard and Thomas Nutter. Richard lay unconscious and still where he had fallen. Thomas was quite alert but unable to get up.

"I think my leg's busted."

A quick examination by one of the Knights, Chevalier Malcolm, who as it transpired was a medical practitioner, confirmed that Thomas's leg was indeed broken. Clearly Thomas and Richard both needed proper attention and as soon as possible. Hector phoned 999 to summon an ambulance and the police.

While they all awaited the arrival of these services, Chevalier Malcolm turned his attentions to Richard who was showing signs of stirring. Hector meantime went into Seaview Cottage to remove his Knight's garb and to check out the surveillance recording. After a quick scan he picked out the key part of the conversation in which DI Huxtable had revealed his guilt. He exited the cottage again and knelt beside Thomas.

"Well Thomas, I've just had a quick look at the laptop and it looks as though you and Richard did a great job getting as good as a confession out of Huxtable. I'm sorry we didn't get here sooner, but we got held up on the road."

"Better late than never." Thomas gave a weak smile. "Mind you; if you had come much later we would have been thrown over the cliff. I'd rather have a broken leg any day."

While Hector had been inside the cottage Professor Macdonald had been talking with Thomas to take his mind off the pain in his leg. As he talked, he shared his puzzlement at the sight of Howard Winkley, the Inverness based university bursar, trussed up as a member of this wholly contemptible criminal gang. His astonishment was the greater when Thomas revealed.

"Oh, didn't you realise, he was Huxtable's accomplice at Sweetheart Abbey."

At this revelation, a police car and van arrived followed a couple of minutes later by an ambulance. Statements were taken from Hector, and Ruairidh. The three bound men were bundled into the police van, while Thomas and Richard were eased on to stretchers, wheeled into the ambulance and whisked to Accident and Emergency in Dumfries.

It was Hector who was able to give the fullest account of events and having noted the salient facts, the officer in charge, sought further statements from others of the curious green cloaked figures that had been present at the scene of the crime. He looked about him, but they and the Lexus had vanished.

Pushing his cap back and mopping his brow, the police officer asked:

"Who were these people who were milling around when we arrived ?"

It was Ruairidh who answered.

"They didn't leave their names, but they were very chivalrous. I heard someone call them The Elven Knights."

Hector gave Ruairidh an old fashioned look.

"Fairy tales Professor! Just fairy tales!"

* * *

That evening Frances was at Richard's bed-side in the Dumfries and Galloway Royal Infirmary. The ward sister had told her that Richard had a nasty concussion, but that there was no obvious sign of brain damage. He was under sedation, however, and not to be distressed.

197

"Oh Richard, what am I going to do with you? Sure I let you out of my sight for five minutes and you end up in hospital. The sister says they're keeping you in overnight for observation, but you should get home tomorrow."

The ex-monk squeezed Frances' hand and smiled.

"Have you heard how Thomas is?"

"Yes, Ruairidh and Hector are with him just now. He has a broken leg, but he'll be out soon too. It looks as though I'll have two difficult patients to keep an eye on over the next while. It's just like old times when I was a nurse. I'm going to be quite strict you know."

Richard started to feel drowsy, but he smiled a wicked smile.

"Oh I like it when you're strict."

He drifted into a deep sleep.

And so, in due course, the two warriors returned to Dalmannoch under the watchful eye of the ex-nursing sister Frances.

* * *

The account given by Thomas of the murder of Colin McCulloch, backed up by the damning video recording, caused ructions within the Dumfries police HQ. That one of their own had been guilty of such a heinous crime was a matter of acute embarrassment to the Chief Constable. Lessons would be learnt. Procedures would be tightened up. In fact, such was Detective Inspector Alexander Huxtable's twisted deviousness, that no procedure could have predicted his evil actions.

His battered body was recovered from the rocks and buried without ceremony in an unmarked grave. Even the Elect of the Revelation failed to send a representative.

It will be no surprise that Bulldog Billy Smith and Sammy (the Sadist) Black were charged and found guilty of conspiracy and aggravated assault. For this they each got five years.

The case of Howard Winkley was a different matter. Apart from his active participation in the Sweetheart Abbey affair, it was discovered that he had also been embezzling substantial sums from the university and not just from the MacPhedran Institute. He was charged with fraud, rape, as an accessory to murder and perverting the course of justice. For this he was sentenced to fifteen years and was put on the Sex Offender's Register. He served but a short part of this sentence for after four months he was found early one morning hanged in his cell.

Of the Elect of the Revelation little more was heard. The sect seemed to disintegrate after the defeat at the Battle of Dalmannoch and the humiliation of four of its prominent members being found guilty of serious crimes. And yes, Howard Winkley was none other than their treasurer who had used his embezzled funds to further the sect's and his own standing. Pastor Erskine Mutch vanished from the scene. It was rumoured that he had moved to the United States and had started a new evangelical church in the Mid-West.

The Elven Knights too receded from public view, but with a renewed inner sense of purpose. Through their recent efforts, they had achieved much success in their mission to protect Galloway's rich and ancient spiritual and cultural heritage and help those unjustly treated by the law. It was decided that, while their ceremonies and activities would remain secret, their existence should henceforth be revealed. The unveiling was to be achieved discretely through publication of Colin McCulloch's researches. The editing was carried out by Angela Trevelyan, with input by Minerva Skinner and all under the joint direction of Professor Ruairidh Alasdair Macdonald and Hector Woodrow-Douglas. It has to be admitted that the relationship between the two women was professional if not wholly cordial.

As for Derrydruie, at an acrimonious council meeting, planning consent for the theme park was refused by a majority of one vote. Sir Crispin Short was declared bankrupt and his estate was put up for sale in several lots. Derrydruie was purchased by a hitherto unheard of trust – The Elven Trust. It may be guessed who formed the board of trustees.

At Dalmannoch something like normality was restored, apart, that is, from Thomas, for a while, stomping around on crutches and a stookie. He tried to make himself useful, but with limited success. However, their shared adventure had created a new and strong comradeship between him and Richard, notwithstanding their very divergent spiritual paths.

There was another deviation from normality. That was the evolving plan for a bigger and more financially viable Dalmannoch. The main manifestation of this was the planned autumn music festival which occupied a good deal of Susie's time aided by Jonathan and several others. The good news in that regard was that the internationally renowned folk singer Donnelly Dolan had agreed to be the headline act and to waive his normally exorbitant fee. Such were Suzie's powers of persuasion. Already bookings were looking promising.

Brother Richard recovered quickly from his own injuries, for, under that gentle exterior, as the professor had said, he was 'as tough as old boots'. In a quiet moment with Frances he confessed:

"You know Francie, the business of Colin's murder and the Elect of the Revelation was pretty action-packed, wasn't it – especially when the Elven Knights got involved. Now that it's all cleared up, it'll be good to have a bit of peace and quiet for a while."

Frances smiled, looked at him, leaned over and gave him a soft and lingering kiss.

"Peace and quiet? Enjoy it while you can my lovely man, because I've something to tell you.

Richard looked at the dark haired Irish woman he adored and wondered what she had in store for him.

"Oh yes? What do you have to tell me?"

She held both his hands in hers.

"You're going to be a daddy."

THE END ?
(Well no. A new beginning)

GLOSSARY OF SCOTS AND GAELIC WORDS AND EXPRESSIONS

The glossary below lists the Gaelic and Scots words and phrases that appear in this book with linguistic differentiation indicated as follows: S = Scots; SG = Scottish Gaelic

Aa (S) All
Aathegither (S) altogether
a' chuain (SG) Of the sea
Aff-hand (S) Off-hand
Agus (SG) And
A Nochd (SG) Tonight
Ain (S) Own
Aw (S) all
Awa (S) Away
Aye (S) Yes
Aye (S) Always
Beag (SG) Little
Brither (S) Brother
Buik (S) Book
Byordiner (S) Out-of-the-ordinary
Cadal Math (SG) Sleep well
Cam (S) Come
Canna (S) Can't
Ciamar a tha sibh ? (SG) How are you ?
Corp (S) Corpse, body
Daein (S) Doing
Dail Manach (SG) Dalmannoch (monks' meadow)
Daoine Sìth (SG) Faerie People, the 'Little Folk'
Daur (S) Dare
Dinna (S) Don't
Doire (SG) (pron. dirra) Wood, glade
Donn (SG) (pron. down) Brown

Doon (S) Down
Doonhamer (S) A native of Dumfries
Draoidh (SG) Druid, wizard
Dug (S) Dog
Eilean (SG) (pron. Ailan) Island
Efter (S) After
Enyuch (S) Enough
Exactly (S) Exactly
Fae (S) From
Fàilte (SG) Welcome
Feasgar math dhaimh (SG) Good evening to you
Fun' (S) Found
Fur (S) For
Gàidhlig (SG) Gaelic
Gallghaidhealaibh (SG) Galloway
Gie (S) Give
Gies (S) Gives
Gin (S) If
Gress (S) Grass
Grunnan (SG) Group, cluster
Gu Brath (SG) (pron. gu <u>brah</u>) For Ever
Guid (S) Good
Hae (S) Have
Hairm (S) Harm
Hame (S) Home
Hauf (S) Half
His-sel' (S) Himself
Hoo (S) How
Hoolet (S) Owl
Jiss (S) Just
Kent (S) Knew
Killt (S) Killed
Lang (S) Long
Lea' (S) Leave
Luggin in (S) Eavesdropping

Losh (S) Lord
Mair (S) More
Mak (S) Make
Michty me (S) an expression of surprise
Mind (S) Remember
Mon (S) Must
Muckle (S) Much, a lot
Nae (S) Not
Nicht (S) Night
Noo (S) Now
O (S) Of
Offski (Slang) Rapid departure
Oidhche Mhath (SG) Good night
Oor (S) Our
Oot (S) Out
Ower (S) Over, too
Polis (S) Police
Richt (S) Right, correct
Ridirean (SG) (pron. <u>Ree</u>jeran) Knights
Sharn (S), Manure
Sith (SG) (pron. Shee) meaning both peace and faerie
Skoosh (S) Squirt, spray
Staine (S) Stone
Stookie (S) Plaster cast
Tae (S) To
Tak (S) Take
Tapadh leibh (SG) Thank you
Thae (S) Those
Thaim (S) Them
Thigibh a steach (SG) Come in
Til (S) To
Traivellin (S) Travelling
Twa (S) Two
Veesitor (S) Visitor
Wabbit (S) Exhausted

Wiel (S) Well
Wi (S) With
Widna (S) Wouldn't
Wiz (S) Was
Ye (S) You
Yer (S) Your
Yersel' (S) Yourself

THE DISSOLUTE COUNCILLOR

A SLEEK BLACK MOTOR YACHT headed purposely southwards through the Sound of Sleat, the waterway that divides the Inner Hebridean Island of Skye from the Scottish mainland.

Viewing the yacht's progress, from Camas Cross on the Skye shore, it was Kirsty Anna Mackinnon who first saw the body floating at the water's edge. At first she thought it was a seal. Then the realisation dawned that this was no seal. She grabbed her boyfriend's arm.

"Oh my God Iain! Look!"

Iain Campbell followed her gaze and saw, partly covered in seaweed, the half-submerged figure of a man, face down, slowly rising and falling in the tide-line wavelets caused by the passing vessel's wash. On closer inspection Iain saw the body. It was that of a middle aged man dressed in a dark business suit. He pulled the body a little up the beach. There was no sign of life

"We'll need to get help. Kirsty. Go up to the house there and call the police. I'll stay here on watch."

Half an hour later the police were at the scene. The young lovers were briefly questioned and then dismissed. The body was later identified as that of Ewan Allan MacLeod, an elected member of the Highland Council.

* * *

Councillor MacLeod had not come home on the two previous nights. He ran a guest house near Broadford with his wife Shona. In truth, it was Shona who ran the business, for Councillor MacLeod was often away in Inverness at Council meetings or locally at the Masonic lodge or who knew where. He had his strengths as a councillor; affable, a persuasive orator and ready to support those in need. Of late too he had also been active and "away" on some "hush-hush" inter-authority group looking at the merits or otherwise of greater political autonomy for the Scottish islands. On the other hand, as a man, everyone knew that he drank too much and when in his cups he could be nasty, aggressive and vindictive. It was quite well known too that he had a fancy woman in Inverness.

Mrs MacLeod was well used to her husband's absences. Inverness was an hour and a half's drive away – two hours if the traffic was bad. When there was a morning council meeting, it was quite usual for Ewan to drive over the night before, or to stay on if he was already there. What irritated her was when he "forgot" to tell her. It was not so much that she missed him, but that the uncertainty spoilt her own plans. Normally he would ring the following day to explain that a special evening meeting had been called, or he had bumped into an acquaintance, had gone for a dram and couldn't drive, or some such.

On this occasion, after a second night without any contact, she had phoned the Council HQ. He had not been seen there that week. She tried the lodge. Again there had been no sign of him there. So they said; although she suspected the brethren sometimes covered up for him if he had been on the "ran-dan".

At midday she rang the local police to let them know that she was becoming concerned. She was reassured that they would put the word out and let her know as soon as they found out where he was. As a public figure Councillor MacLeod was of course well known to the police.

For the rest of the day she busied herself with the duties that befall a guest house proprietrix. As she did so she thought about her lot. They had not been blessed with children, but they were comfortable enough financially. When they were young Ewan had been good-looking, witty and as elder brother stood to inherit the croft on which the guest house now stood. When Ewan's parents had assigned the croft to them, the young couple, with a generous grant for the then Highland Board, built the guest house alongside the old croft house. The latter remained the home of Ewan's parents until they passed away. It was now a self-catering holiday cottage producing a useful income. Yes they were comfortable enough and she enjoyed the status of going to civic functions as a councillor's wife. It was just that Ewan had gone to seed and they had grown apart.

She thought of Ewan's younger brother, Donald Angus, a different kettle of fish. As a young man, he had been in Ewan's shadow, with it seemed lesser prospects. He went to sea, saw the world and eventually gained his mate's ticket. Then he got the call to the ministry and was ordained as the Reverend Donald Angus MacLeod with a church way down in the rural far south west of Scotland. He had married Jessie a happy-go-lucky farmer's daughter and now they had five lively children.

From what she had heard, while by no means well off, they had a happy and fulfilling life. Donald Angus was far removed from the oft-caricatured straight-laced, sanctimonious West Highland preacher. Larger than life, he was an accomplished piper and leader of a group of Gaelic learners based at some sort of cultural centre called Dalmannoch. He seemed to have struck up a rapport with the manager there, a former Catholic monk called Brother Richard.

A television programme on BBC Alba the week before had featured Dalmannoch as the venue of a music festival that seemed to have attracted a large, weird and wonderful collection of folkies, New Agers, Pagans, Christians and not a few 'normal' individuals. And there on screen was the burly and bearded Donald with dog collar and pipes under his arms extoling, in his fluent native Gaelic, Dalmannoch's creed of sectarian tolerance. To Shona, it seemed like another world.

These thoughts were banished by the arrival of a couple of Germans on tour by motor cycle. They had been booked in by the tourist information centre. These were followed in due course by the usual mix of visitors – English, Dutch, Japanese plus the two electricians from Glasgow, booked in for two weeks to upgrade a local sub-station. Each were shown their quarters. There was the meal to prepare and serve and advice to be given as to local events, beauty spots and sites of interest, of which there are many on Skye.

Late that evening two uniformed police officers, a male and female, rang the front door bell. Shona MacLeod opened the door and could tell immediately by the grave expression on the officers' faces that something serious was afoot.

"Mrs MacLeod, I'm afraid I have some very bad news."

"Come in. Please come in."

She showed the two officers into the dining room, for there were still guests in the lounge.

"Mrs MacLeod, I'm Sergeant Steven Nicolson and this is WPC Gillies. I think it would be best if you sat down,"

She did so.

"I'm afraid your husband's body was found earlier today in the sea, by the shore at Camas Cross."

Shona MacLeod said nothing, she was stunned.

The police woman put her hand on Shona's.

"I'm sorry."

For a time Shona was silent.

"What happened?" Why . . . ? Oh God!

The officers allowed time for the awful truth to sink in and then the police woman spoke again.

"Councillor MacLeod's body has been taken to Inverness for *post mortem*. We need you to come to identify the body. If you would be so kind."

"What tonight? *Mo chreach* ! I have guests in the house. I've . . ."

"No, no not tonight. Of course not. We can take you tomorrow by police car."

And so it was that Shona MacLeod arranged for her neighbour, Ann Henderson, to cover for her in the guest house and set off with heavy heart, after breakfast, the following morning for Raigmore Hospital in Inverness. She drove her own car rather than be stuck in the company of the police for a whole day.

She presented herself at reception as arranged and was accompanied to the morgue by an Inspector MacGillivray for the harrowing process of identification. There was no doubt. It *was* Ewan. The inspector then asked her to follow him by car to the Burnett Road Police Station. The shock of confirmation of her husband's identity was compounded by the inspector's surprise revelation.

"Mrs MacLeod, I'm afraid I have to tell you that a *post mortem* has been carried out on Councillor MacLeod and it seems that the cause of death is strangulation and that this happened before his immersion in the sea. We are treating this as a case of murder."